"What? Didn't think I had the brains to do it?" she asked.

A burst of air left Nate's mouth, sounding like an annoyed half laugh, and he shook his head. "No, Carly, I didn't say a thing."

She crossed her arms. "You may not have said it, but you thought it."

"And just how would you know what I thought?"

"Because you have that look on your face. Superior and all-knowing. And you're male. All men think the same thing—that women are incompetent creatures who rely on a man's input for every single thing."

Nate stared at her a moment as if he had no idea what planet she came from, then put up his hands in surrender. "I concede. You're right—"

"Aha!"

"I *am* male. But I have no idea what you're talking about or where you get your ideas."

PAMELA GRIFFIN lives in Texas and divides her time among family, church activities, and writing. She fully gave her life to the Lord in 1988 after a rebellious young adulthood and owes the fact that she's still alive today to an all-loving and forgiving God and a mother who prayed that her wayward daughter would come "home." Pamela's main goal in writing Christian romance is to encourage others through entertaining stories that also heal the wounded spirit.

Please visit Pamela at www.Pamela-Griffin.com.

Books by Pamela Griffin

HEARTSONG PRESENTS

HP372—'Til We Meet Again
HP420—In the Secret Place
HP446—Angels to Watch over Me
HP469—Beacon of Truth
HP520—The Flame Within
HP560—Heart Appearances
HP586—A Single Rose
HP617—Run Fast, My Love
HP697—Dear Granny
HP711—A Gentle Fragrance
HP720—A Bridge across the Sea

Don't miss out on any of our super romances. Write to us at the following address for information on our newest releases and club information.

Heartsong Presents Readers' Service
PO Box 721
Uhrichsville, OH 44683

Or visit www.heartsongpresents.com

Long Trail to Love

Pamela Griffin

Heartsong Presents

A special thanks to Therese Travis and Adrie Ashford for their invaluable crits. And to my Savior, who protected and led me down the long trail to eternal life, I give You my all.

A note from the Author:
I love to hear from my readers! You may correspond with me by writing:

Pamela Griffin
Author Relations
PO Box 721
Uhrichsville, OH 44683

ISBN 978-1-59789-617-7

LONG TRAIL TO LOVE

Our mission is to publish and distribute inspirational products offering exceptional value and biblical encouragement to the masses.

PRINTED IN THE U.S.A.

one

The telephone's shrill ring interrupted Carly's conversation with Leslie and Jill, her best friends and the only two people in Goosebury who would have anything to do with her at the moment.

"Aren't you going to answer it?" Leslie asked when the insistent bell clanged through the room a third time.

"No." Carly pursed her lips in disgust. "Why should I? It's him. I know his ring."

"His ring?" Leslie shared a look with Jill.

"Okay, maybe that sounds crazy, but he hasn't stopped calling since Mrs. Vance caught us arguing in the park two days ago." *And heard every disparaging, condemning word aired.*

"You weren't to blame, Carly," Leslie soothed. "We know that. No one thinks any less of you for what happened."

Carly knew better. "I feel as if everyone in town has branded me with some sort of scarlet letter. In line at the post office this morning, two old women were whispering. They mentioned my name and kept darting glances my way. And yesterday when I popped into the news office to see if you wanted to do lunch, everyone looked at me, then became real busy, though a few told me 'hi'—nervous 'hi's,' I might add."

"I think you're seeing things that aren't there." The gentle flow of Jill's Australian accent helped soothe Carly's nerves, nerves the jangling phone attacked as it rang once more. "You did used to work there, and after that row you had with Abernathy, I imagine they were surprised to see you. Don't worry about what others say or think. The bush telegraph will judge how it wants to in any case, and that's the way of it—the town gossips," she inserted when Carly looked at her stupefied. "Once news of a more shocking nature comes along, this will be forgotten."

"You're right, Ju-Ju," Carly said with a wry twist of her lips. "The vultures will gather once a new corpse has been found in someone else's closet. What about you?" she asked Leslie. "Does Dear Granny have any pearls of wisdom for me today?" She gave a rueful shake of her head. "If I'd just taken your advice, I might not be in this jam." Leslie had often spoken to her about God in the year and nine months they'd known each other. In her top-secret profession as Goosebury's advice columnist to the lovelorn, Leslie gave biblical advice with the aid of her grandmother, advice that at first annoyed Carly. However, as the months progressed, she and Leslie looked beyond their differences and became good friends. Carly had known Jill less than half that time, but they, too, had become close.

Leslie's eyes held sympathy. "I think Jill's right on with this one, Carly. Nobody at the office has been gossiping about you, not to my knowledge. And if a few old ladies have nothing better to do than to run people down, well, that kind of thing has been going on for centuries. Don't let it get to you; it's not like you to get so upset."

Frustrated with the entire situation, Carly swept the receiver up as it shrilled a seventh ring—"Hello!" Warmth crept over her face at the stern greeting she received. "Oh, hi, Aunt Dorothy. . .No, he's not home yet. . .Okay, sorry about that. . . Yes, all right, I'll tell him."

"That was my aunt," she needlessly explained as she hung up the phone. "She wanted to know if my uncle Michael was home."

"See, you worked yourself up over nothing," Leslie gently chastised. "Jake has probably given up chasing you."

"You don't know how much I've wanted to change this phone number these past two days!" Carly groaned and slumped to a chair. "Always having to sprint for the phone before my family could pick it up hasn't been easy. My aunt must know about Jake from all the gossip—I'm amazed she hasn't confronted me with it yet. But if she knew he was calling me, still trying to see me. . ." Carly sighed.

"Can't you just explain matters to her?" Leslie asked.

"Are you kidding? My aunt wrote me off as a bad seed the moment they took me in. She's always treated me as the unwanted child; not that I care. I don't." She ignored the prick in her heart that told her otherwise.

"Why didn't you just bail out once you came of age?" Jill asked.

"I should have, but life intervened. The year I graduated, I'd planned on getting an apartment with a classmate, but that was also the year my aunt got sick with the tumor, so I stuck around here to help out. Trina was too young to do much for her mom or take care of the house, and I felt obligated since they'd given me a place to live. My uncle hasn't been so bad, but my aunt sometimes looks at me as if she hates me."

Carly knew the reason for the woman's hatred but didn't voice it, still ashamed by what her aunt said her mother did all those years ago. Before Carly even knew of such things, Aunt Dorothy had claimed that a mother's sins became the daughter's and had placed Carly in the same despicable class as her mother. If Aunt Dorothy learned of this situation, everything she'd ever accused Carly of would be justified.

Leslie broke the silence. "I've talked to Blaine, and we've decided to move into my loft and rent out his house. We don't need two places, especially since they're next door to each other. Would you be interested?"

Carly smiled at her friend's thoughtfulness; she'd never

understood how Leslie could be so tolerant toward her, when she'd been so undeserving of her forgiveness during those first months Leslie started work at the *Goosebury Gazette*. Blaine had been something of a landlord to Leslie before they married, and both shared the trait of a protective attitude toward others.

"If I still had my job, I'd jump at your offer, Les, but I have no income to afford my own place. I am a complete dolt—what's that word you use, Ju-Ju? For a fool that's duped?"

"A mug." Jill looked sympathetic.

"Yeah, that's what I am. A mug."

"Since Mr. Abernathy is my boss and has married my grandmother, I could put in a good word for you," Leslie suggested.

Carly winced at the memory of her last outburst at the *Gazette*. Over a year ago, when she'd first discovered Jake's lies, she had created a scene while conducting an interview. Her boss had given her a fiery tongue-lashing but also a second chance. Always restless, and unhappy at the *Gazette*, she'd wanted to quit then but had needed the income and couldn't find another job that suited. This last time when she'd learned she'd been deceived, while taking a phone call at the office, she'd had a meltdown and Abernathy had had enough.

"I doubt I'll get good references from the Big Chief," Carly said. "Or a third chance. And anyway, I don't want to get you involved in my problems."

"You're my friend. That makes me involved already."

Carly didn't know what she'd done to deserve these two, but she was grateful for friends like Leslie and Jill.

"Say. . ." Jill's blue eyes looked thoughtful. Carly had seen that expression enough times to recognize her friend was cooking up a plan. "Some of my mates from church are joining me and Ted to hike up the Long Trail into Canada in two weeks. You're between jobs and want to distance yourself from

Goosebury until things cool down. Why not join us?"

At the word *church*, Carly inwardly cringed. Ironic that her two best friends in the world were Christians, since Carly wanted nothing to do with Christ. "Will there be a lot of preaching?"

"We'll hold a Bible study and have devotions each night before we turn in, but we won't tie you to a tree and force you to attend, Carly."

Carly chuckled at the sparkle in Jill's eyes. She'd never been on the Long Trail, though she'd promised herself she would attempt the extensive hike someday. As she listened to Jill gush about the exquisite scenery, the scope of mountains, and the experiences she'd shared with her husband when they'd section-hiked the trail, an idea came to Carly. She had made a living as a writer. Maybe she could document her experience and write a guidebook for beginners by a beginner. That idea might reel in the readers, especially those interested in the outdoors.

Still, she hesitated. "Is there a list of items I'd need? I can't invest in anything extra right now."

"I'll get you the list tomorrow. Anything you can't afford, I might have a spare. Ted and I have done a lot of hiking over the years, so I have heaps of gear. You can have my old tent—it's ace, not a thing wrong with it; we just needed a bigger one after we married." Jill fairly bubbled with enthusiasm. "You'll only need what you can carry in a backpack, along with a pair of good sturdy shoes. The sporting goods store is having a corker of a sale from what I saw in an ad this week, so no worries there, either. And you'll have plenty of time to break them in. Oh, this is exciting! Ted's bringing his mate along, and now I'm bringing mine."

"Ted's bringing a friend?" Carly felt her internal radar go on the alert.

"Oh, no worries about Nate. He's fair dinkum."

"Uh, yep, I'm sure he is." From her experience, Carly doubted any guy was genuine or trustworthy.

"You two are making me jealous," Leslie complained with a sad chuckle, putting a hand to her six-months-pregnant stomach. "I would love to go hiking. It seems as if it's been forever since Blaine and I went anywhere, even to visit covered bridges."

"Oh, poor you." Jill threw a semi-mocking glance her way. "If I could, I'd exchange places with you in a heartbeat."

Leslie's face reddened, and remorse swept over Jill's features. "Oh, Leslie, I didn't mean that the way it came off."

"I know. But you're right. I should count my blessings instead of complaining about what I can't have."

Sensing unease in the atmosphere, and knowing Jill's frustration stemmed from being married five years and not having the child she desired while Leslie became pregnant within three months after her marriage to Blaine, Carly voiced her decision.

"All right, Ju-Ju, you've convinced me. I'll invest in a pair of hiking boots and take that 270-mile journey down the long, long, *Long* Trail."

They all laughed, but restlessness still coiled deep inside Carly.

Knowing Jake, he would make another appearance in Goosebury soon, determined to see her. He hadn't given up the first time, and she doubted he would retreat this time either. She needed to get as far away from him as possible. The next two weeks couldn't go by fast enough.

❧

Nate stuffed as few articles in his backpack as he felt he needed for the month-long hike.

"So you're really going then?"

At the unexpected voice, he jumped and turned toward his door. His father stood in the entrance. At Nate's look of surprise, he explained, "I knocked, but the door was ajar."

Nate gave a short nod. He must not have closed his apartment door all the way when he'd come home, loaded down with shopping bags. The air currents in the outside corridor had a habit of pushing the door open if it didn't stick, but his frustrations didn't end there when it came to this place. He really needed to find somewhere else to live, but it was the only place available in his price range when he had been looking. Still, if a reporter and not his dad had been standing there, Nate would have been cornered.

He eyed his father in his gray suit with navy tie, his silvering hair distinguished and brushed back from his face in a confident manner, his entire appearance calculated to assure clients he remained the man in control. But today his father didn't look in control. New lines creased his brow, and a defeated hunch bowed his shoulders.

"Dad, I just need some time alone. To put distance between myself and Bridgedale and to sort things out."

"She wasn't worth it, son. I know it hurts, but any woman who won't stand by her man doesn't merit the money it takes to pad her lifestyle. You're better off without her."

Nate sensed that, but the reminder didn't help right now. He had thought he might propose to Susan once upon a time but had held back. Now he was glad he had. Losing his job, several of his so-called friends, and his girlfriend within a twenty-four-hour period had been tough. Dealing with the newscast that sent his family's life whirling into upheaval would have been that much more difficult if Susan had thrown his ring back in his face, too. Nate retrieved his camera from a shelf and stuffed it inside its protective carrier. He planned to take plenty of pictures while he connected with nature and, he hoped, rediscovered the peace that notoriety had wrenched from his life.

"Your stepmother is heartbroken. I don't know what to tell her. I never had a teenager become so rebellious, and I have no idea what to advise her concerning Brian."

Nate's jaw clenched. The last thing he wanted to talk about was his felon of a stepbrother or the social-conscious woman who sucked his father dry of funds at every chance she could. Rail about the two of them, yes. Maybe that would ease the frustration packed inside him like a time bomb ready to go off. But seeing the once-proud attorney reduced to such a torn, humbled man twisted Nate's heart, and he withheld his true feelings.

"I'm sure you'll work things out, Dad. You always do."

"This, I'm afraid, is beyond working out." His father took a seat on Nate's bed and shook his head.

Nate sympathized with his father, but he'd heard once that an empty vessel didn't do much good at filling others' pots, and his was as dry as a bone. None of the Bible promises he'd read during his long-ago studies seemed to float to mind, and he hoped that these weeks away would improve his connection to his Savior. Lately, he felt like the line between them crackled with static.

"I can't say I blame you for leaving," his father said. "The media can be merciless, but Julia wanted to stay close—though after that sad excuse for a preliminary hearing and the mob bearing down on us like baying hounds on the courthouse steps. . ." He sighed, breaking off his thought. "I was afraid she might have a breakdown. I should have taken her on a cruise months ago. Since my last client dropped me, I don't know why I don't." He bowed his head into his hands. "She blames me for not representing Brian, though I've told her I'm not a criminal attorney. Even if I were, I couldn't act in his defense because of the conflict of interest."

"Maybe you *should* take that cruise. You need some peace, too." Nate clapped a hand to his father's shoulder in a show of support, all he could offer at the moment. "I'll be back long before the trial starts. I'm not running out on you."

"You've always been dependable, son. I know I can count on you. Your mother would have been proud."

The reference to his mom made Nate think of his sister, a mirror-image to the first Mrs. Bigelow. "At least Nina lives in Connecticut and is immune to all this."

His father slapped his leg in frustration. "It just isn't right. You shouldn't have been made to suffer so; none of this was your fault."

"Yeah, well, life's not fair. Never has been, never will be." Nate shrugged into his backpack, adjusting the strap. "But we have to struggle along and make the best of things somehow— isn't that what you always told me?"

His father let out a dry chuckle. "I never knew you were listening."

"I always listened."

The two men shared a look charged with emotion, each of them letting the other know without words that he was important.

"Just don't make the same mistakes I did, son."

Nate gave a slight nod. "I'll keep that in mind, Dad."

two

A short trek from the road where the bus dropped them off led Carly and her group to the state line bordering Massachusetts and Vermont, the beginning of the southern boundary of the trail. In the hazy sunlight, under a covering of beech trees, the group assembled. With walking sticks in hand, they toted backpacks and looked like the serious hikers they would need to become. Carly studied the other six in the group, a man and his daughter, a newlywed couple, and Jill and her husband, Ted. Ted's friend hadn't shown up, which made Carly breathe a sigh of relief.

A rugged wooden sign with painted yellow letters marked their welcome onto the Long Trail, calling it "A FOOTPATH IN THE WILDERNESS." Instructions underneath offered helpful information on the painted blazes marking the path—white for the main trail, blue for side trails. Below that came information on the Green Mountain Club, the organization that had created the trail decades ago. Carly took a picture of the sign with her camera, thinking she would want to supply photos for the guidebook she planned to write.

Ted Lizacek, Jill's husband and leader of their motley group of seven, stood with his hands on his hips and eyed them with all the aplomb of a drill sergeant mustering his troops. His stint in the army had had lasting effects, apparent in the rigid set of his jaw and shoulders and in his no-nonsense demeanor. "I hope everyone here has spent the past weeks conditioning for this hike. The trail starts out easy but gets rougher as the days progress. A good thing, too. It'll strengthen those leg muscles and get you sluggards into physical, mental, and emotional shape. Once we hit the north end toward Canada, the hike becomes more difficult. The terrain gets treacherous and will involve a lot of climbing, sometimes requiring hands as well as feet. The path is always rugged. It's not for the faint of heart."

Across from Carly, a pretty blond teen with thick glasses that magnified sky blue eyes shot an anxious glance toward her father, a man of similar coloring. He gave her a reassuring wink, but his smile seemed faint.

"What a way to rally the troops, luv." Jill put her hand to Ted's back. "If you don't curb your welcoming speech, it might turn into an address of farewell. This isn't like when we traveled into the outback. At least we'll reach shelters on this trail, and signs are posted so we can't get lost."

Carly heard a deep, quiet chuckle behind her and looked over her shoulder, startled. A pair of blue-gray eyes in a bronzed, masculine face caught and held her attention. The owner of the eyes looked in her direction, and she turned her head back around so fast she almost gave herself whiplash. She pressed her hand to the burn zipping along her neck. Great. The last thing she needed was a muscle spasm. She wondered where he'd come from; she hadn't seen him on the bus.

"It's important that everyone understands the difficulties we'll come up against," Ted countered.

"Which is why we gave out detailed information weeks ago, and I'm sure everyone has read their brochures by now," Jill mollified.

"All right, maybe I went a little overboard."

"A little overboard?" Carly heard the man behind her mutter in amused disbelief. "Try more like taking a bungee jump off a high cliff." She felt her lips twitch but kept her focus on their hiking leaders.

Ted straightened, evidently having heard his heckler. His gaze speared the man behind Carly. "Well, well, well. You got something to say, slacker? Come out from hiding and speak up so everyone can hear."

Like an unruly child facing a stern instructor, the man stepped out from behind Carly, and she got her first good look at him. Slim and well toned, he wore a blue plaid shirt with the sleeves ripped off over a long-sleeved gray flannel shirt and blue jeans. Sandy brown hair hung shaggy and windswept to his nape, feathering in soft waves in a long sweep over his forehead and angling in shorter waves at the sides. He stood several inches taller than her five foot six. Realizing she stared, she shifted her attention to Ted, who crossed his arms across his barrel chest.

"What have you got to say for yourself, boy?" Ted addressed the man as if he were years younger, though Carly thought they appeared near the same age.

"Well, now," the stranger spoke with unhurried ease, "I thought I'd signed up for a pleasure hike along the Long Trail, not a grueling, thirty-day workout at Ted Lizacek's Boot Camp."

Uncomfortable silence filtered through the group. All Carly could hear was the wind rustling the leaves and the sounds of other hikers in the distance as they readied for their departure.

Ted's eyebrows shot up. "Something wrong with that idea?"

"Maybe not for a PC game or for one of those so-called reality shows. As for real life, I think I'll just stick to enjoying this hike—minus the drills, Sarge."

Ted glared at the unflappable man seconds longer before bursting into laughter and slapping his heckler on the back. The mock tension broke as they smiled at one another. Carly shook her head, realizing their little joke.

"Nate, man, it's good to see you! When did you sneak in?

Everybody, Nate here is my old hiking buddy. We section-hiked this trail for the first time together when we were juniors in high school."

"And you were just as overbearing then as you are now," Nate said good-naturedly.

"Yeah, but you wouldn't recognize me any other way," Ted joked back. "I want you to meet the group. Jill, you know."

"G'day, Nate," she said, giving him a hug. "Good to see you again."

"And this is Kim and her dad, Frank Melby," he addressed the teenager and the man beside her.

Nate shook the man's hand and gave the teen a smile and nod. Carly noted his even, white teeth made the smile swoonable, which would explain Kim's pink face.

Swoonable? *Man, I've been out of a job too long. I'm getting rusty in my vocabulary. Maybe I should create a dictionary of ridiculous adjectives and try to sell that.* Before she could break from the thought, Nate moved to stand in front of her, his steady, blue-gray eyes making contact with hers. She drew a swift breath, which she quickly related to embarrassment at just connecting Nate to her crazy new word for the day.

"Nate, this is Carly Alden," Jill said, an undertone of exuberance that hinted of matchmaking, evident where it had been absent in previous introductions. Carly shot Jill a warning glance, then looked back to Nate.

"It's nice to meet you," she said in a noncommittal manner.

His smile edged up a notch at the corners, suggesting he also heard the undertones and they amused him. "Likewise."

She pulled her hand from his warm grasp and averted her gaze to the next available face. It turned out to be Jill's, and her traitorous friend had the audacity to wink.

Ted and Jill continued down the line with introductions, with Nate between them. Needing time alone to sort out her thoughts and knowing Ted intended to start the hike soon, Carly took the opportunity to sign the register.

Maybe coming on this hike had been a mistake, but she had to avoid any chance of running into Jake again. He wasn't the type to tolerate waiting for long; nor was he the type to accept rejection. He pushed the buttons and expected everyone to hop when he said hop. Given that he was CEO of his own company, his attitude wasn't much of a surprise.

Her mind switched to Nate, and she observed him without his noticing. He laughed at something Frank said, and turned to Bart, the other guy on the hike. She'd heard only good things from Jill about Nate for the past two weeks without really learning anything personal about the man. That alone made her skeptical. She wondered if she was the only one in the group who found it odd that Ted or Jill hadn't introduced Nate by his last name. Maybe because the three were friends, they missed the fact others wouldn't know it. Not that she cared one way or the other. The less she had to do with the male species, the better, and at the first opportunity, she would stress that fact to Jill. As for Nate, the absence of his last name aided Carly's desire to keep him at arm's length.

After more than an hour on the bus, her muscles felt cramped, and knowing their supercharged drill sergeant was eager to get started on the twelve-mile hike to the first shelter, Carly set down her backpack and stretched her legs with slow, easy lunges. Her body was well toned thanks to daily aerobics, and she'd spent the past weeks walking every morning and evening, increasing her mileage each time to prepare for what promised to be a grueling but stimulating month.

"Hi!"

Carly turned to see Kim smile as she approached. In her gray sweatshirt bearing the name of a well-known pop group emblazoned in pink across its middle, and with the remnants of baby fat pleasantly rounding pink cheeks, the girl looked thirteen or fourteen.

"Hi." Carly straightened from her stretch.

"Can you believe this day finally got here?" Kim's bright features matched her eager words. "I thought it would never happen. I've been putting red Xs on my calendar forever!"

"I take it you're just a tad excited?" Carly joked.

"Well, yeah!" Kim laughed. "I mean, this has been like a dream of mine ever since I was little and heard how my grandparents hiked the trail when they were young. I read that not everyone makes it. Since the trail first opened in 1930, only about twenty-six hundred hikers have made it to Canada—at least I think that's how many." Kim pulled her eyebrows together. "Anyway, whatever, a lot dropped out along the way because they just didn't have the strength and endurance needed. But I'm going to make it—me and my dad."

Carly smiled. "I'll bet you are, Kim, and I'll be rooting for you all the way."

"Hey, thanks. You, too! Well, I guess I'll talk to you later. I know Mr. Lizacek wants to go soon." With a slight wave, Kim returned to the group.

Carly liked the exuberant teen. So far, everyone seemed like they would make good companions for an extended hike. They hadn't started preaching to her the moment they saw her, as she had half-suspected they might, and she'd found common ground with a couple of them. The newlyweds, Bart and Sierra, shared her lifelong love of historical Native American culture and art, and they'd conversed during the bus ride. Carly and Jill were good friends, despite differences in their beliefs, or rather Carly's lack of one. And though she and Ted never talked much, he always treated her with respect.

She looked over the group, her attention going to the newcomer. With a start, she noticed Nate looking at her. She thought she read a sort of watchful amusement in his eyes but realized, from a distance of at least thirty feet, it was impossible to tell.

She broke eye contact. Well, at least *most* of her group seemed like they would make good companions. Uneasy, she turned her back to Nate and continued her warm-up lunges, her defensive nature waving warning flags inside her mind.

❧

Four miles into the trail, Nate began to relax. The stress from the upcoming court case and his family situation eased away the deeper he forged into the endless tunnel of greenery. A mix of abundant hardwoods, towering evergreens, and copious overgrowth that spanned the entire length of Vermont, the thick forest traveled along the spine of the Green Mountains.

He took deep breaths of the bracing air, rich with the earthy aroma. An earlier rain sharpened the scent. Today's hike wasn't strenuous, but Nate knew he wasn't in the same shape as he'd been the last time he and Ted had hiked this trail. Not that he was out of shape, but riding his tour-guide cart around on his last job hadn't been physically challenging.

Carly, who ambled ahead about ten feet behind Frank, suddenly stopped and aimed the camera hanging around her neck toward one of many trees. Nate knew that Ted wanted to reach Congdon Shelter and get situated before dark. They were behind schedule, and this had been the third time Carly had stopped to aim her digital. Nate came up beside her.

He looked in the direction she aimed, at the tree on which a ring-eyed furry observer perched. "You might not want to use all your shots our first day out. You'll see plenty of raccoons and much better scenery farther up the trail."

She lowered her camera. Her night-dark eyes seemed to glimmer with contained steam. "Maybe, but I won't see *that* particular raccoon again." She raised her camera and compressed the shutter.

O-kay. Nate studied Carly, not sure what to make of her. By her body language—the haughty tilt to her chin and the straight set to her shoulders—he sensed her hostility but didn't understand the reason for it. He'd tried to be nice to everyone, but she seemed to want no part of his company. Not that he looked forward to anything other than friendship these upcoming weeks.

Her sleek hair was almost coal-black, and she had pulled it high into a ponytail that brushed the center of her shoulder blades. Her khaki shirt set off the olive tones in her smooth skin, complementing her exotic beauty, whether Latina or Native American, he wasn't sure. Incredibly full lips that rimmed a large mouth above a more delicate chin with high cheekbones did nothing to detract from the appealing picture.

"Yes?" Clearly miffed, she turned to catch him staring. "Was there something else?"

Maybe her exotic blood originated from the Arctic, what with the frost he was getting.

He decided to shrug off her attitude. "We should catch up to the others. It looks as if we're going to get more rain before this day is through, and that'll slow us down."

"Don't let me stop you." She pushed a button on her digital camera to view her shot.

"Well, see, that presents a problem." He knew she wouldn't like what he had to say, and he respected her obvious independent nature. But he also knew this was the church group's first time on this particular trail, and they were unfamiliar with what to expect.

"Really?" She regarded him with a sort of lofty disdain as if he were a black fly she'd like to swat away.

"Yes. I told Ted I'd help out when he first invited me to come along, and he asked if I would take up the rear during our hikes."

"Okay?" she inquired impatiently, waiting for him to elaborate.

"Well, if I leave you behind, that pretty much takes away my designated spot."

"In other words, don't be a slacker?"

He couldn't help but grin. "I wouldn't put it in Ted's words, but that's the gist of it."

"Okay, fine, whatever." She shut off her camera.

"We just want to keep everyone together and don't want anyone lagging too far behind. They have those white blazes to mark the trail, but it's still possible to get lost."

"No problem. I understand." Her terse words showed her irritation, but she began walking.

It didn't take a woodpecker drilling the info into his head for Nate to figure out he wasn't welcome company to Carly, but if he stayed behind her and walked any slower, he would be taking baby steps. Still, the need to walk single file impressed itself upon him, so he moved in closer, hoping to speed her up a little. She shot him a glare that stifled anything further he might have said.

Withholding a sigh, he dropped back a few feet. The trail had been aptly named—this was going to be one long hike.

three

Near Seth Warner Shelter, Jill convinced Ted to stop for a lunch break. They were halfway to their night stop, but Carly had a feeling if Ted could have gotten away with it, he would have continued the remaining six miles and forced everyone to chow on granola bars and trail mix while they plodded ever onward.

"Everyone needs a breather," Carly heard Jill tell her husband. "You're used to a heap of physical activity, but this is their first day out. We need to call it quits, or someone could strain a muscle."

Ted gave in with reluctance, and Carly mentally applauded Jill. Carly had practiced carrying her forty-pound backpack when she trained on the lane near her home, but she'd never carried one for so long, and her shoulders and lower back burned. A break to sit and rest would be welcome, and as the others dropped their backpacks and walking sticks on the ground with relieved sighs, Carly knew she wasn't the only one who thought so.

Her gaze wandered to Nate. A flush of embarrassment shot through her to see him look up from setting down his pack to catch her watching him. She looked away.

Since their slight altercation, Carly had worked harder to push ahead, walking faster, though after a couple of miles, her shins and thigh muscles complained at the mistreatment, and she acknowledged her foolishness. She couldn't explain her irritation with the man, since Nate had only followed Ted's orders in watching out for those green to the trail, but felt her unease had something to do with how Nate stared at her. She darted a glance his way. He was still staring at her.

She took a seat on the platform of the three-sided shelter, which was damp, but she'd been forewarned that rain and getting wet were givens on this hike. Retrieving a package of freeze-dried vegetable crunchies from her backpack, she also pulled out her mini recorder to recount her first day on the trail so far. The all-encompassing forest of greenery refreshed her soul, as did the scent of rain.

Sierra joined her, asking what she was doing. When Carly admitted her former job as a journalist and that she wanted to compile information for a book, Sierra asked questions regarding writing and the publishing business, stating that she'd thought about submitting some poetry to a publisher. The two talked until Ted rallied everyone to resume the hike, and the break ended.

Instead of relieving her aching muscles, the rest had made them feel worse. Carly groaned as she slipped on and buckled her backpack around herself.

"The first days are hassles," Jill sympathized. "It'll get better once your body adapts to the new routine."

Carly hoped Jill was right and only the first days were bad; no matter how hard she tried to keep to the front, her flaming shins and aching lower back had her lagging toward the rear, until she again trudged in front of Nate. She felt his eyes burn through her scalp, and she lost her footing. Her arms flew out as she struggled to regain her balance.

Nate grabbed her arm before she could fall in the mud. "Watch out for those tree roots."

"Thanks." Her face flushed hot, but she didn't make eye contact with him.

The remaining miles awkward, Carly forced herself to concentrate on the tree-lined view and the path while thinking of ideas to add to her book. By the time they reached Congdon

Shelter, gray clouds loomed above, shot with orange from the evening sun. Ted instructed the group to pitch their tents before the deluge hit, and Carly hurried to do so, pleased that regular practice in her backyard now had her looking like a pro. Satisfied, she straightened and brushed off her hands, noticing Nate watching from several feet away. He'd already pitched his tent about fifteen feet from hers.

"What? Didn't think I had the brains to do it?" she asked.

A burst of air left Nate's mouth, sounding like an annoyed half laugh, and he shook his head. "No, Carly, I didn't say a thing."

She crossed her arms. "You may not have said it, but you thought it."

"And just how would you know what I thought?"

"Because you have that look on your face. Superior and all-knowing. And you're male. All men think the same thing—that women are incompetent creatures who rely on a man's input for every single thing."

Nate stared at her a moment as if he had no idea what planet she came from, then put up his hands in surrender. "I concede. You're right—"

"Aha!"

"I *am* male. But I have no idea what you're talking about or where you get your ideas. And the look on my face was admiration for how fast you put that tent up. Jill told me this was your first time camping overnight."

Carly felt a niggling irritation that Jill had spoken to Nate about her. "I've been on day hikes before. And I've camped out at cabins."

"Not exactly the same thing."

Carly couldn't argue with that. At least the shelter had a privy—but not much else.

A smattering of raindrops struck her cheek and head, and she looked up at the same time Nate did.

"You better duck inside your tent," Nate said. Then as if sensing her bristle, he added, "Just a suggestion if you don't want to drown. Not an order."

"Drown?"

"Never mind."

The faint smile on his face as he moved to his own tent needled her, but she resisted the urge to demand an answer. She ducked into her tent and zipped it closed. With hardly enough room to move, she decided against cooking one of her one-dish meal packets on her portable stove, choosing instead to eat nuts and dried fruit for dinner.

The rain splattered against her tent, then slammed into it in a deluge.

"Carly!"

Surprised to hear someone outside, she unzipped the partition partway. Jill stood in a rain slicker and handed her something.

"Heyo. I brought you a prezzy I thought you could use."

Thunder rocked the trees behind as a zigzag of lightning flashed through the sky. Carly undid the zipper all the way and pulled Jill inside the cramped tent.

"Are you nuts? You shouldn't have come out here in this!"

"This? This is nothing. One thing about weather and the trail—you can't wait out the weather, or the weather will outwait you."

"Huh?"

"Something Ted said. The weather always changes, and on a hike like this, you're the one who has to conform. I've been in worse Down Under. Heatstroke and bush fires aren't something you want to tangle with, though a small bush telly would come in handy right about now!" She shrugged, laughing. "I came to bring this. It's exceptional for sore muscles."

Carly unscrewed the top from the tube of ointment and

flinched as the heavy menthol odor infiltrated her nose. "Oh! Between that and the bug repellent, I'll be a candidate for the worst-smelling hiker on the trail. Then again, maybe I should patent the combination. I might have come up with a great new scent guaranteed to repel men—Keep Away."

Carly laughed, and Jill shook her head at her silliness.

"It is bad, but you won't regret using it. Ted won't go on hikes without it."

"Ted?" Carly's picture of the strong, unflappable outdoorsman didn't include an image of a man with aches and pains.

"Too right! For all his bluff and bluster, he's oversensitive when it comes to sickness or pain. All men are, from what I've seen." Jill winked and smiled, making Carly laugh. "But Ted is also one of the best mates I've known, an ace leader, and smart when the need arises. He may be gruff on the outside, but he's really a big koala bear and one of the nicest blokes I know. I was filming the roos, and he swept me off my feet—after he smashed into my Jeep."

"I remember months ago you told me the story of when you met in Australia, but I forgot all of it."

"I was doing a nature film, a hobby I had, filming home movies, and out of nowhere Ted came barreling into my life. You should have seen him, Carly. At first I thought he had a few kangaroos loose in the top paddock." She tapped her head. "He kept yabbering an apology, then invited me out to dinner. At first I steered clear—I thought he was a big galoot. But later I realized he wasn't such a bad bloke, after all."

"Too bad there aren't more guys like Ted filling the earth," Carly mused.

"Nate's blood is worth bottling." At Carly's lost look, Jill laughed. "I mean he's an ace bloke—and helpful, too."

Carly shot her friend a warning look. "Not interested, and I really don't think there are any ace blokes." She realized her words might offend. "Well, except maybe Ted. But my uncle's a loser, my dad—whoever he is—is a loser, and of course it goes without saying that Jake was."

"You can't generalize the entire male population into 'loser' status, Carly. It's not fair to good men like Nate. Give him a fair go. Just as a good mate—a friend—nothing else."

"Why should I? I'm not here to start a new relationship. I'm here to escape an old one. Partly. I also wanted to gather info for a book, but I told you about that. And that's all I want, so please don't try to hook us up."

"I'm not suggesting that." Jill let out a soft breath. "I understand your reasons, but I hate to see you close yourself off when someone as beaut as Nate is around."

"Jill. . . ," Carly said in warning.

"Okay." Jill put her hand up as if making an oath. "Even though it goes against my wish to see two of the nicest people I know become good mates, I promise not to interfere."

"Thank you."

"I better get back before Ted thinks I made a boat and sailed away. Get some good sleep. Oh." She stuck her hand in her pocket as if just remembering something and pulled out a handful of sweets. "Want some lollies?"

Carly took a cinnamon disk. "You're going to get cavities with as much candy as you eat. I'm surprised you took up room to pack them."

Jill left laughing, and Carly settled down for the night.

As the rain pummeled the weatherproof tent, she reflected on their conversation. Jill had vowed not to interfere, but remembering the tone of her voice, Carly became uneasy. Jill wasn't the type to go back on her word, but Carly sensed her friend had something up her sleeve.

❧

Nate couldn't figure Carly out. After the incident at the shelter, he resolved to steer clear of her. Yet as their second day on the trail progressed, he found himself watching her more than he should. Of course, since she was often the one to lag to the back of the line, that wasn't hard to do.

The climb up Harmon Hill wasn't so bad, and the clear view of the green valley refreshed them after all the rain, but from there, the trail made a steep descent by means of a natural stone staircase that seemed to go on forever. Another cross over Maple Hill and then another descent further challenged tired muscles.

Because of the shelter spacing and the need for water, they had to hike fourteen miles that day. After they'd been on the trail a number of hours, Nate could see Carly lagged even more, and he reduced his pace. He opened his mouth to ask if she needed a rest, then thought better of it. He felt relieved when Ted broke for lunch once they reached Hell Hollow Brook. An anomaly to its name, the water rushed clear and refreshing over smooth rocks of all shapes and sizes. Abundant fronds of tall greenery bordered the narrow brook, reaching almost to touch at the center in some points.

His friend looked as weary as the greenhorns to the trail, and Nate held back a chuckle. The first few days were always the toughest in hiking a trail like this one, but it satisfied Nate to see their robust and vital leader struggle with the same problems, since he had bullied them so.

"Guess that's not a very Christian attitude," he muttered to himself. "I shouldn't wish upon my team leader the same pains we're all having."

Carly stopped and turned. "What?"

"Nothing," he said, surprised she'd heard him. "I wasn't talking to you. I was talking to myself."

She gave him a skeptical, accusing glance. He shook it off and took a seat beneath one of the maple trees on a smooth boulder, one of many that filled the trail. This one felt surprisingly comfortable. He took a long draw from his water bottle and squinted against the sunlight as he watched Carly take a spot yards away under another group of trees. Kim joined her, and Carly smiled, her attitude friendly.

At least she opened up to the other hikers, though Nate noticed she never went to them. They always came to her. As she tossed back her long dark hair, which she'd pulled out of a ponytail, and threaded her slim fingers through it, Nate dwelled on the enigma of Carly. Did she think herself too good for everyone, or was she shy? No, not shy. And with the amenable and laughing conversations he'd witnessed between her and Jill, her and Sierra, and now her and Kim, he didn't think she thought herself superior to anyone, either. Yet for all that, she still seemed to hold herself aloof, as if she bore an invisible sign that said, TRESPASSERS WILL BE SHOT. And she'd made it abundantly clear Nate fit into that category.

He shook his head, reconciled to the idea, and concentrated on tearing his teeth into his beef jerky while appreciating the scenery. Fog hovered above the trees in the distance. He hoped they wouldn't get more rain.

Seeing the water in his bottle was low, Nate squatted down by the creek to refill it, dropped in a water purification tablet, and screwed the lid back on. Hearing a stir in the grasses behind him, Nate looked over his shoulder.

"Thought you had a good idea," Ted explained, unscrewing his own water bottle. He struggled to get down so he could submerge the bottle, and winced. Nate felt bad about his earlier vengeful enjoyment that they were going through mutual aches and pains.

"Trail getting to you there, buddy?" he joked.

Ted snorted. "Don't tell the others, but I'm not exactly as young as we were when we hiked it in high school."

"Really? Never would have guessed. The way you were leaning on your walking stick, I just thought you were trying it out as a pole for a high jump."

"Yeah, ha ha, very funny. I'll be twenty-nine in a few weeks, but today I feel like fifty."

"Twenty-nine isn't so old." Nate grinned. He was two years younger.

"Thanks," Ted said dryly. "I guess it wouldn't be so hard if Jill wasn't wanting a kid so bad. I do, too, but not as much as she does."

"Did you talk to a doctor? You said you were going to."

"Yeah, both of us are okay. Not sure what the holdup is."

"Well. . ." Nate used his walking stick to help him straighten. Today his shins burned like crazy. "You're always telling me God's plans don't fit into our timetables, so maybe that's all it is. It's just not time yet." He shifted his gaze to the right and felt a jolt of shock to see Carly staring at him. She looked away, back to Kim.

"Could be." Ted straightened, following Nate's gaze. Nate detected a smile in his voice. "You know, it wouldn't hurt you to settle down. Plenty of nice girls in Vermont to choose from. Some right under your nose."

Nate swung his head around to see Ted grinning at him like a maniacal Cheshire cat.

"Yeah, well, the interest has to work both ways. Don't want anything one-sided."

"Maybe it does."

"What are you talking about?"

"What are *you* talking about?"

Nate wasn't about to fall into that trap. "What I felt you were talking about."

"Don't you mean who I was talking about?" His focus went to Carly. "She's a real looker; likes the outdoors, too. And you're sharing the same trail for the next month. You couldn't do better if she were hand-delivered to your door."

Nate snorted. "Except for one small point."

"What's that?"

"She has no interest in me."

"I doubt that."

"What makes you think she does?"

"I've watched her watch you. People not interested don't stare."

Nate thought that over. "Maybe she's plotting my demise."

Ted grunted and rolled his eyes. "When did you get so stupid? You were always smart in school."

Nate decided to let that one go. "What do you know about her?"

"Not much. She's Jill's friend—met her at a vegetable stand of all places. But she's nice. And she's had a rough time. Her ex-boyfriend did her wrong, but that's all Jill told me. I think the real problem is that you represent the entire male community in her mind, and right now, she's targeted man as her enemy."

"I noticed that when she talks to you, she doesn't look like she's plotting where to hide your body."

Ted laughed. "Yeah, but that's because I'm spoken for. I don't represent a threat to her. You do."

"I try to be nice."

"It has nothing to do with nice. You're young, single, and out looking."

"I am not out looking. I just broke up with Susan, remember. Or anyway, she broke up with me."

"Buddy, before marriage, every man is out looking, whether he'll admit it or not. You may not know you're looking, but tell the truth. When you meet a girl who attracts you, isn't one of the questions going through your mind, 'I wonder if she's the one?' And I'll bet you thought that about Carly, too."

Nate didn't want to admit Ted was right. At twenty-seven, with most of his former classmates married, he'd thought a lot about settling down. He'd wondered if Susan might be the one, before three months of getting to know her and discovering what she was like. From knowing Carly two days, he didn't even need to ask the question. Without a doubt, she wasn't the one for him. They couldn't exchange a few sentences without her thinking he harbored ulterior motives.

"I think maybe you need something more than water purifier tablets," Nate muttered. "Some microorganism must have gone to your brain and made you a little nuts."

"Mark my words," Ted said, walking away with a chuckle. "By this time next year, you may just be asking me to be your best man."

"Make that *a lot* nuts," Nate called after him as he walked behind Ted.

"You want some nuts?" Jill asked, coming up to him. "I've got chocolate-covered peanuts."

"Thanks." Too embarrassed to correct her as to what he meant, Nate accepted a handful and ignored Ted, who was laughing so hard he sounded as if he might come apart at the seams.

four

The farther they walked through this part of the trail, now thickly wooded and giving off a feeling of extreme isolation, the more grateful Carly was for her walking stick—though every so often, the staff became stuck in the slurping mud and she had to pull it out. The traction on the bottom of her heavy hiking boots helped her keep her footing on slippery ground, and two pairs of socks prevented blisters. But at times she longed for the freedom of bare feet. Still, the positives outweighed the negatives.

Earlier the group had taken several levels of stairs up the Glastenbury fire tower to see the sun paint the Taconic Mountains with early morning gold, and Carly hadn't been disappointed. Staring at such an impressive vista, Carly could almost believe God existed.

"Look!"

Kim stopped on the path and turned sideways, her pink face alight. Carly followed her gaze to see a small porcupine bristle through the undergrowth.

"Look at it walk," Kim giggled. "It waddles like an overblown pincushion on rickety wheels."

Carly smiled. It did look funny. She grabbed her camera and readied it, then noticed Nate come up beside them.

"Permission granted?" she asked dryly, not failing to see Kim's blue eyes widen behind the lenses of her glasses.

"Whatever." Nate gave a grunt mixed with a less than amused half smile. "Don't get too close, Kim," he warned the girl, who'd also taken her camera out and edged closer to the trees as the porcupine waddled away.

"I was just hoping to get a shot from the front," Kim explained, disappointed.

"Better safe than sorry. If you advance, you might scare it into thinking you're a predator. And you don't want to get on the wrong end of a porcupine's quills. They're loose, and if it lashes out its tail, it can hit you, embedding the quills in your leg like darts."

"Too bad I don't have quills to lash out and discourage advances from predators of the two-legged variety," Carly muttered under her breath once Kim resumed walking.

"What?" Nate turned a sharp glance her way.

"Nothing." Carly smiled sweetly and continued her trek. "I wasn't talking to you. I was talking to myself."

"Sure you were," she thought she heard him say but didn't look back to ask. She chuckled under her breath, so busy giving herself a mental two points that she didn't think to step around the large puddle like Kim had and instead sloshed right through it. The tip of her clunky hiking shoe caught on a tree root hidden beneath the inches-deep muddy water, and she went sprawling forward to land hard on her hands and knees.

Nate came up beside her. "You okay?"

"Yeah. Just dandy." Embarrassment that he should see her in such a humbled position put a bite to her words. She moved her hands to get better traction, but the mud and the weight of her heavy backpack made her slide forward, drenching her shirt even more.

He held out his hand. "Need a lift up?"

"No." She gritted her teeth. "Thanks. I can do it myself." This time she planted her hands in front of her and pushed her right foot forward to boost herself into an upward lunge. Despite the traction of her sole, she slipped hard and fell farther into the mire with a splash. She spit out muddy droplets in disgust.

"You're doing a great job of it so far."

She heard the thread of amusement in his voice and glared. "Don't you have anywhere else to go, or do you get your kicks out of annoying me?"

His eyebrow arched, and she felt a moment's remorse. She knew he was only trying to help, but her pride stung worse than her body. Had anyone else witnessed her dilemma, it might not have wounded so bad, but that it was Nate made it feel like alcohol on a cut.

"Just. . .please. Go. Really, I can handle it."

"Suit yourself."

His light words and merry whistle as he walked off didn't surprise her half as much as the fact that he'd actually left her alone on the trail. Sure, that was what she wanted. But what happened to his claim of needing to take up the rear to watch over any laggers? She guessed he wasn't as sincere or genuine as Jill had tagged him.

Planting her walking stick in the sludge and using it as a brace, Carly struggled to her knees and finally to her feet. With care, she stepped out of the puddle, then surveyed herself, letting out a heartfelt groan. Her whole front looked as if she'd been dipped in a vat of milk chocolate. Maybe if it were milk chocolate, it wouldn't be so bad. Of course, the bugs might then feast on her despite the noxious repellent she wore.

She took the bend on the trail and stopped in surprise.

Nate stood off to the side, his camera focused on the summit of Glastenbury Mountain, just visible through the trees.

"Glad to see you made it okay," he murmured.

Suspicious, she studied him, not failing to notice the slight quirk of his lips when he turned and took in her appearance.

"I thought we weren't supposed to loiter behind and take pictures along the trail."

"That was only because of the rainstorm. No danger of rain on the trail right now. . .though of course there's always danger of getting wet."

She wanted to remain aloof, but his deadpan words struck her as funny. She could feel the corners of her telltale mouth edge upward in a smile. Astonishment swept over his face before she turned away, resuming her trek.

"Speaking of water, the sooner I find a body of it to immerse myself in—preferably clean water—the better."

"Don't take it so hard." He fell into step beside her. Here the trail was wider, though most of the time they had to walk single file; the pamphlet Jill had given her said that to prevent erosion, hikers should stick to the middle. She opened her mouth to remind him, but he spoke before she had a chance.

"Falls are a natural part of life when hiking. Skinning knees, scraping hands—I imagine every one of us will do it many times before we reach Canada. Shedding a little blood is a given with as rough as this trail can get."

Strangely, his quiet words reassured her, didn't make her feel so awkward or humiliated, and she cut him a glance.

"I think the worst for me was when I fell down some rocks and scraped one side of my face and side. For days, I wasn't a pretty sight—unless you like red, black, and purple as a color combination."

She took note of his profile, his straight nose, and his strong, lean jaw. His skin had undergone a slight burn, especially the bridge of his nose and his cheekbones, but was unmarred. She couldn't imagine him unattractive. When she realized where her mind had taken her, she forced her attention away from him and onto the hike.

He fell back into step behind her, and she wondered if he had just remembered the single-file rule or if he had given up trying to steer her into conversation. Regarding Nate, Carly felt nonplussed and uncertain, and she didn't like anything that threatened her independence and self-control.

❧

A few nights later, Nate grew reflective as he gathered with the others in a circle, using the remnants of the flaming sunset for light. Of all the summits they'd crossed, the one today was a favorite of Nate's: Bromley Mountain, with a spectacular view of the landscape in all directions.

Fire rings were allowed at some camps, but the wind blew too strong that evening to build one. Nate relied on his slim pocket flashlight once the red and gold in the western sky gave out. This was the first evening they'd reached the shelter early enough to set up camp and still have time for group devotions before sunset. The shelter housed eight, and five new high school graduates occupied it, so Nate's group had needed to pitch tents. After the other young men and women introduced themselves, they dove into their sleeping bags and zipped themselves in, exhausted. This had been the first evening Nate's group hadn't just wanted to let their aching bodies tumble into their sleeping bags after having said a communal prayer of thanks for making it to their destination alive and in one piece yet again. At long last, they felt acclimated to the hike.

Nate flipped to the seventh chapter of Romans in his pocket Testament and listened as Ted's strong voice seemed to shake the air as he read. A snapping twig diverted Nate's attention to the trees across from him. Carly stood at the edge of the clearing, her stance rigid.

He watched her until she turned her head, her gaze meeting his. The same jolt of awareness hit as it always did when they seemed to connect. Then to his disappointed frustration, she turned on her heel and walked back to the shelter and, he assumed, the latrine.

He had trouble concentrating on the discussion afterward,

but he made a monumental effort to keep his focus on the topic.

"I find it interesting how Paul said he always wants to do what's good, but he winds up doing those things he doesn't want to do instead." Kim let out a sigh. "That makes me feel better. To know someone like the apostle Paul dealt with messing things up, too, well, I don't feel like such a hopeless case. So I guess the question I have is this: What was his secret? How did he overcome all that to be able to be so strong in prison and through all those beatings and the torture?"

Amazed, Nate stared. He had never figured the bubbly teen, who giggled constantly and talked about pop bands at all the breaks, would have so much depth.

Jill smiled at Kim. "I think the answer is that we must build our spirits, put the ol' flesh man to death—the one that always hassles us and craves sin. The only way we can tackle that is by spending significant time in God's Word and in prayer."

Nate listened with half an ear. Carly came into view again, and he focused on her, waiting for her to rejoin them. He was surprised when she went to her tent instead.

"Jill's right," Ted said. "This hike is a great chance to get in tune with our Creator and get closer to Him. I encourage all of you to do that. I like to pick a time of day when I can be alone and just go off a short distance to look at the mountains and meditate on God."

"So then, we *can* wander from camp?" Kim sounded puzzled. "I thought that we're supposed to stick together. Especially after we saw that sign on the road."

Everyone grew quiet. Nate recalled the sign that the U.S. Forest Service posted with photographs of two backpackers who'd been killed and an appeal requesting the public's assistance in identifying the perpetrator.

"Everyone needs some time alone. Just don't stay away long

or go far. No more distance than a half block. Tell someone before you go that you're leaving, as well as what direction you're heading. And always take your backpack. That way you'll have your compass, your flashlight, and anything else you might need."

"You mean if we get lost?"

"You shouldn't get lost if you don't go too far." Ted's words became abrupt, a sign he now felt boxed in by Kim's worried attitude. He had never developed good people skills.

"Why do you think they call this Lost Pond Shelter?" Bart asked, not helping matters any. "You think someone got lost here once? I read on a Web site there have been people who signed the register and took the trail but were never heard from again."

"Thank you, Major Suspense," Sierra joked, rolling her eyes.

"What?" He looked at his wife. "I'm just curious."

"Kim." Jill's voice was gentle. "Whenever you need to take some time off, give me a nod, and I'll walk with you most of the way." She looked at her husband. "Since you, Nate, and I have taken this trail and all the others are new to it, I think we should use the trail-mate system in such cases."

"Assign all the greenhorns expert buddies?" Ted wanted to know.

"We could do that." Jill nodded. "I'll be stuffed; I'm not sure why I didn't think of it before. That sounds like a corker of an idea."

"I'd like to be assigned to Kim," her father said. "I've had experience hiking along the Appalachian Trail."

"Sure, Frank." Ted gave a nod of consent.

The young newlyweds shared a smile, and Bart winked at his wife. "We'd like to be trail mates," he said, turning to Ted.

"I think," Jill observed, "since you're both new to this trail, it would be better if I take Sierra, and Ted takes Bart."

"That sounds doable," Bart agreed.

"So, I guess that leaves Carly for Nate."

Hearing the words jarred Nate, though he saw it coming the minute the topic had switched to assigned buddies.

"That okay with you, partner?" Ted asked.

Even in the dying light, Nate detected the amused glint in Ted's eyes. Thinking of the curt treatment he'd already received from the independent spitfire, he sent Ted a look that promised payback.

"If it's okay with Carly. Sure."

Sending a resigned look to her tent, he wondered who would convince *her* of the new plan.

five

Once Carly buried all remains of breakfast—a preventive measure to keep from attracting animals—she brushed her hands off on her canvas walking shorts and looked up. A quiet groan escaped when she saw Nate headed her way. Couldn't the man just leave her alone for once?

"Yes?"

"Good morning to you, too," he responded cheerfully despite her abrupt greeting.

A hint of embarrassed warmth flashed over her face. "Morning," she mumbled, heading back to her tent to finish packing up.

"If you have a moment, I'd like to talk to you."

She sighed and turned around. "Yes?"

"Last night, the group decided to employ the buddy system."

Mystified, Carly eyed him. "The buddy system?"

"Where no one goes off alone, but everyone travels in pairs."

"I do know what the buddy system is." She hoped she had been assigned to Jill, but from Nate's uneasy behavior, she suspected the worst.

"Great. And, well"—he spread his hands wide—"you're looking at your new trail mate."

Terrific. First she'd ripped the packet of her granola and blueberries cereal too fast and too wide, spraying the contents of her breakfast all over the ground; next, she'd been attacked by swarming black flies during her latrine run because she'd forgotten to apply her bug repellent; and now this. The start to a perfect morning.

"Thanks, anyway, but I'll pass."

"Well, it's not exactly an option."

"I don't need an escort. I can do fine on my own."

"Everyone has a trail mate. It was Ted and Jill's idea."

She would just bet it was Jill's idea! "Maybe so, but I don't need one. I've done some camping, and I do know enough not to go wandering off and get lost, contrary to the helpless female you think me to be."

"What I think you to be?" He shook his head as though flummoxed. "How did this get into a discussion of my hypothetical opinion of you as an individual?"

She shrugged. "That's what it amounts to, doesn't it? Even if you don't come right out and say it, you think I can't cope."

"I never said—"

"Oh, you don't have to say it. You've got it written all over your face. So, are you one of those men who think a woman's only place is at home, preferably at the stovetop or in whatever room happens to interest him?"

"*What*? How did you come up with that?"

"Never mind. You don't have to answer if you don't want to. I understand. Personal views tend to put people in sticky situations."

He settled his hands on slim hips and studied the treetops as if trying to find his bearings, shot her a baffled glance, shook his head, and walked off.

A smidgeon of remorse niggled a hole in her triumph. Jake and her uncle did hold such outdated views; she and Jake had fought about it. But maybe she shouldn't have been so hard on Nate since she didn't know him or his personal opinions. On the flip side, if she kept pushing him away, he might soon get the message and not be inclined to pursue her to "buddy up."

Frustrated, Carly used unnecessary force to roll her sleeping bag and fasten it to the backpack. No man could be as "ace" as

Jill claimed Nate was; the man was sure to have his faults. No admirable man existed on the planet. Not Jake, not her uncle, not even her father, whoever he was. . .though sometimes she felt she knew.

She stopped packing and grew somber, staring at the trees without seeing them. Her high school beauty-queen mom had gotten pregnant as a senior, given birth to Carly, then two years later dumped her off onto her childless married sister with the explanation that she needed to go and "find herself."

Carly wondered if after twenty years her mother had found herself yet.

༚

They hiked down to Big Branch River, where a suspension bridge stretched across and led into an extensive clearing. From there, they began a gradual climb up to Little Rock Pond. Nate smiled when Jill and Sierra oohed and ahhed over the peaceful area with its tranquil waters, so clear they could see all the way to the bottom of the deep pond. Rimmed by low mountains covered with thick forests of trees, the pond invited weary travelers to rest, and the women asked if they could. Ted agreed and called an early lunch.

"From this angle, it's mysterious," Kim said, "almost gothic, with the way it's hidden and protected in shadow, like something you might see in England or Scotland."

"Have you ever been to either of those places, Kim?" Nate asked.

She gave a self-conscious grin. "No, but I've seen pictures."

"I agree," Sierra said. "It gives off an aura of mystery, especially with the mist. It inspires a poem; if I had a few hours, I'd give it a shot."

"What about you, Carly?" Noticing she'd taken a seat a few feet away on a partially submerged boulder at the edge of the pond, Nate attempted to pull her into the conversation. "What are your views of Little Rock Pond?"

She looked away from the pond and unscrewed the top of her water bottle. "It's nice."

Nice. Well, what should he expect after the silent treatment she'd given him all morning? At least she'd spoken those two words to him. She acted as if he was the one responsible for incorporating the buddy system into their group—which Nate considered a good idea, regardless of what Carly thought. He just had no idea how this trail-mate idea would pan out; somehow, he had to find neutral ground with her these next few weeks.

After their break, they made a short descent before climbing the summit of White Rock Mountain. A downhill spur led them to the awe-inspiring White Rock Cliffs. They climbed to the top, and Nate watched Carly move toward the edge.

"You might want to drop that heavy backpack before getting too close," Nate suggested.

She shot him an annoyed look but did as he said.

The cliffs plunged straight down into a sunlit valley, with distant peaks beyond. When Carly's shoe sent some loose pebbles plummeting over the edge, Nate barely restrained himself from grabbing her arm and instead only murmured, "Watch yourself."

She didn't answer, and he worked to bury his impatience with her attitude; this silent treatment was really getting on his nerves.

The rest of the day went much in the same manner. Clarendon Gorge, with its steep descent and narrow suspension bridge that swayed in the wind, had been dedicated to a hiker who'd met his end there before the bridge was built. Carly drew close to the edge to peer the eight hundred or so feet to the rocks and creek below. Did the woman have a death wish? Nate clenched his teeth to prevent himself from calling out words of caution.

Hungry for real food, they made a short detour that led to a popular restaurant for hikers.

Nate wolfed down his steak and eggs. He noted Carly equally enthused about her vegetable salad and shook his head at her food choice but noticed she didn't hesitate to order strawberry shortcake for dessert. So, she had a sweet tooth. He ordered the same, and their eyes met across the table a moment, before she pretended extreme interest in a children's coloring menu left on the table by the last patrons. It wouldn't surprise him if she picked up a crayon and played connect-the-dots to avoid a conversation with him. Noticing a blue crayon by the salt shaker, he was tempted to hand it to her.

At their prearranged food drop, they loaded their backpacks with supplies that should last them until the next place. Those who wanted to made phone calls and mailed letters and postcards to family and friends. Nate wondered how his father was handling the situation at home, but that brought his spirits low, and he concentrated on the reason he'd come here: to get away from the outside world and all its problems.

Once they resumed their trek, the climb became extremely steep; the path led out of the gap and resembled a rockslide, with ferns hanging from cracks along the stone walls. The high humidity didn't help, either.

Nate regretted the full meal he'd eaten, and from the groans he heard, he wasn't the only one. Even Ted set a slower than usual pace. By the time they reached Clarendon Shelter, everyone felt hot, exhausted, and sweaty. Little daylight remained, and Nate found himself in a funk. His sole desire was to stock up on water, pitch his tent, grab some chow, and dive deep into his sleeping bag for an early night.

He crossed the far-reaching carpet of green grass that fronted the three-sided shelter and left his heavy backpack there. Setting off for a nearby stream, he experienced a dark gratitude to be alone. He groaned when he saw Carly had arrived there first. Hearing him, she turned and shot him a suspicious look.

"Are you following me?"

"Why would you think that?" About at the end of his limit, Nate didn't feel up to Carly's verbal jabs.

"Because it seems whatever I did today, you were always behind me, breathing down my neck."

"Maybe if you exercised a little more caution, there wouldn't have been a need."

She frowned. "I was fine both times; I knew to be careful on the summit and the bridge. And I don't need a buddy."

"You say that, but—"

"I do have a brain, you know. I'm not a complete ignoramus."

Nate gritted his teeth. "So you've told me."

"But with the way you act, it's like you've got some misguided, outdated concept that you have to play valiant hero to my helpless heroine. Only I'm not helpless, Nate, contrary to your narrow-minded opinion of me and probably of all women in general."

"I never said—"

"I mean"—she gave an exasperated upward sweep of her hands—"you're always lurking in the shadows, as if this buddy-system thing has gone to your head. Even before that, you were watching my every move like you planned to rush in and cart me off to safety at the least little slip. Well, guess what? I don't need saving! I did great before I met you, and I can do fine on my own now, too."

Seconds of silence crackled between them before Nate swooped down and grabbed her beneath the knees, his other arm looping around her shoulders. He swept her off her feet into his arms. Carly gaped at him, too stunned to speak. Held close against his strength and warmth, his compelling stare drilling her, she found it hard to move her tongue to speak. He straightened, his blue-gray eyes burning inches away from hers.

"Good, it worked." His smile came grim, determined. "I had a feeling this was the only way I could shut you up long enough to actually listen to what I was saying and not just hear what you wanted to. First off, I have the utmost respect for women and don't think they're a weak-kneed, unskilled sex as you're always accusing me. Second, I've never once said a deriding word about you or how I feel about you, and contrary to what you think, you cannot read my mind."

"What's third?" Her voice cracked in a whisper.

"Third?"

"There's always a third."

"You want a third? Okay, here it is—the buddy system stays intact whether you and I like it or not. And unless you can learn to shed some of that prickly independence and not always bare your teeth at a hand offered in friendship, then lady, you might find it hard to keep your feet on solid ground." He set her down hard as he said the last, and her soles hit the soil with a thump.

Immediately, he stepped away, and she pitched sideways, working to catch her balance. She gaped at him like a grounded fish, her eyes bulging, her mouth wide open.

Good. She seemed to have gotten the message.

Without another word, he retraced his steps to the shelter, deciding he would refill his water bottle in the morning.

six

All night, the wind had howled through the trees, but the morning dawned mild. Fog shimmered in the sunlight, cloaking the area in damp mist. Nate hunched down at the brook as he refilled his water bottle, and allowed the breeze to blow away from his mind the clutter of yesterday's fiasco. For the first time in a week, he had snapped, reacting instead of thinking. Now that he'd had time to cool off, he regretted his impulsive actions. If Carly had disliked him before, she must now rank him high on her ten-most-hated-men list.

Hearing a twig snap, he looked over his shoulder. Carly approached, a silver packet in her hand. From the way her gaze darted to him, to the water, then back again, she seemed uncertain.

"Good morning," she said at last.

"Good morning." Nate wondered if she was deliberating giving him a push into the creek.

"I, um. . ." She brought her hand forward with the silver packet. "I brought you a peace offering. I didn't have any of Jill's candy, so I made do with this."

Nate took the protein shake, eyed it, then her. "Thanks." Feeling uneasy but thinking he should take a sip, he did so, trying not to grimace. A recollection of his youth flashed across his mind. He'd never excelled at board games, and his older sister and her friends had taken advantage of that, letting him join in when they played. They made the loser drink a "death drink" composed from any and all contents of refrigerator and cupboards that they could find to make the taste as appalling as possible. Nate always lost. Years later when they were teens, Nina confessed how she and her friends cheated to get Nate back for always tagging along.

Looking at the silver packet, he wondered if and how Carly had managed to filter grass and dirt through the hole with the straw.

"It's not much." She shrugged. "I had some left over when we got to the food drop."

He could understand why.

Before she could walk away, he spoke. "About last night." She looked at him, and he sighed. "I was way out of line, and I'm sorry. Maybe not so much in what I said, but with the way I said it and what I did."

"I had it coming."

Her answer shocked him. He never knew what to expect from her.

"I came on this hike, fresh from ending a relationship that went very sour very fast."

"Sorry to hear that."

"Yeah, well, it wasn't your fault or anyone else's. You've been nice no matter what a grouch I've been. So, I'm sorry, too."

Nate could think of a few occasions when he'd made a comeback, saying something he shouldn't have, but at the thought of peace between them, he decided not to bring them up.

"Anyhow." She nodded to the silver packet in his hand. "You'd better drink the rest if we're going to be trail mates and you plan to keep up with me." Her lips curled into a smirk before she headed back to camp, and he wondered if her words were deliberate and she knew exactly what sacrifice she asked of him in drinking the brew.

He also wondered if squirting the awful-tasting contents into the creek would kill any of the fish. Maybe he was over-dramatizing; he took the barest sip to find out if he'd imagined it. Less than a minute later, after making sure Carly wasn't watching, he emptied the contents of the brown shake onto the ground, then folded the packet and put it with the rest of his garbage he would take with him so as to leave no trace that he'd been there.

He hoped the concoction wouldn't kill the grass.

After a short morning prayer, the group set off for their seventh day on the trail.

A gradual uphill climb near the summit of Beacon Hill and passage through open fields gave Nate a chance to talk to Carly, which he hoped might spur a friendship. Despite her tendency to withdraw to a corner, she possessed an independent, free-spirited quality that drew Nate to her.

"So, tell me," he said as they approached a high ridge above a brook that sparkled with the few coins of sunlight the trees allowed through their branches, "is there part gypsy in your blood?"

Carly laughed, and Nate thought it nicer than any sound he'd heard on the hike thus far. Now that she relaxed around him, she was pleasant to be with.

"Gypsy? No. Nothing Bohemian about me except for some of my clothes. According to what little my aunt has told me, I'm supposed to be descended from an Abenaki chief who made his home in these mountains centuries ago."

Nate studied her proud bearing and exotic features. The idea of Native American princess fit her well.

She looked at the trees. "I think I would have liked to have experienced life back then, but only for a few weeks, maybe a month. I'm too attached to home appliances to want to have lived in historic days."

"Well, you seem to be doing okay without electricity."

"Don't get me wrong—I love it. Like I said, a few weeks in the wilderness is great, and the length of this hike is perfect.

Those packet meals aren't half bad, though I miss cooking from scratch. And the protein shakes were a good investment, too."

A wash of warmth swept up Nate's face, having nothing to do with the exertion of the hike. "Uh, yup."

"If nothing else, they make great fertilizer."

He shot her a sharp look at her wry words. Busted. He shook his head. "How'd you find out?"

"Nate, even the few guys I know who avoid meat wouldn't drink that stuff. Could be because of the alfalfa grass or maybe the kelp. Who knows?"

He stopped in shock. "Kelp? Meaning the green algae that grow at the bottom of ponds?"

She gave him a sweet smile and walked ahead.

"And don't horses eat alfalfa?" So she *had* been trying to feed him grass! "I knew you were trying to kill me," he muttered softly enough so that only she could hear.

She didn't look back, but her laugh brought about a reluctant smile.

❧

The next day took them to Killington Spur. A steady rain started, and everyone decided it best to forego the climb to the second-steepest summit in the state and head for a popular inn for skiers and hikers. To the group's deep gratitude, Ted had made previous reservations, and all were eager for a short overnight stint to wash off the trail dust—or in this case, trail mud—and take a breather. They all knew that the farther the trail went on toward Canada, the more difficult it became, and it had already proven a challenge.

Close to evening, they arrived, weary and beaten, at a charming lodge with gleaming hardwood floors and a convivial stone fireplace in the cheery common area. Each went to their assigned rooms. Once in hers, Carly threw her backpack off, stripped down to nothing, and stood under a hot shower for a good ten minutes. The stress and pain of days on the trail melted away as the reviving needles of water did their magic and massaged tense muscles. Carly released a deep sigh of pleasure, shampooing her hair three times until she felt completely clean. She knew the results wouldn't last, but it was nice to get all the dirt off for at least one night.

Afterward, relaxed and refreshed, she changed into a T-shirt and clean hiking shorts—her only clean clothes—promising herself she would do her laundry before bed. Right now, her stomach growled. She headed to the main part of the lodge to meet with the others for dinner, not all that surprised when Nate alone rose from the sofa in the community area. He'd also showered and changed into a soft plaid shirt, a dark green one with long sleeves rather than the usual torn ones.

"Where are the others?" Carly asked.

"The newlyweds are in their room, Kim wasn't feeling well, and Ted and Jill went off to find a phone and run a few errands."

"So, in other words, it's just us." The last three words gave Carly a strange tingle in the pit of her stomach.

"Looks like it. You hungry?"

"Famished."

"Then what are we standing here for? Allow your trail mate to come to the rescue—just this once." He gave her a mischievous grin and crooked his elbow in a formal manner she'd seen in old movies. She chuckled, relaxing as she took his arm. They found a table for two, and a waitress gave them menus.

"The corned beef with cabbage looks good. . . ." Nate trailed off at the look Carly gave him. "Sorry, I forgot you don't eat meat." He glanced at the menu. "No salad here, either. We can go somewhere else, if you'd like. There's a pub nearby that serves food."

"That's okay. I do eat more than salads." Carly thought it sweet of Nate to offer. Maybe she had pegged him wrong. He really wasn't such a bad guy, but it wasn't until he'd swept her off her feet the other night—literally—that he'd rattled some sense into her brain so she could see it. The memory of their close encounter made her cheeks hot, and she closed the menu.

"I think I'll have the French onion soup and the stuffed mushrooms. Two appetizers should fill me up." The one vegetarian entrée loomed too far out of her price range.

"I still can't believe you fed me grass."

Carly laughed. "Perfectly-good-for-you grass, it was, too. Not a thing in the world wrong with it."

"If you're a horse."

She giggled again at his sober teasing, and conversation flowed easily. Once they gave their order and the meal came, he bowed his head in silent prayer, and she glanced out the window, a bit uneasy. She had realized he was a Christian like the others the night she'd spotted him with his Bible at the group's evening prayer rituals—or whatever they did. But he hadn't tried to shove its contents down her throat at any time this past week or point and call her a sinner, and that helped her to relax. Jill's friends were a lot different than she'd thought they would be. It felt good to be around them.

"So, Carly, tell me—what's your story?"

"My story?" She set down her spoon in the soup bowl and raised her eyebrows. "Now you're the one sounding like a reporter."

He stopped short of taking a bite of his sandwich and peered up at her. "You're a reporter?"

Did she imagine it, or did his words seem tense? "I was. With the *Goosebury Gazette*, our town paper. I handled the entertainment section, current events, that sort of thing."

"Oh." He took a hefty bite, but she sensed something still troubled him. "So, what's Goosebury like nowadays? I lived there a couple of years during high school but don't remember that much about it."

She gave a sharp laugh, capturing his attention again. "Sorry. This isn't the best time to ask me that question. Any other day, I'd say it's your usual charming New England small town, filled with its covered bridges, scenic spots, and the like."

"And on the other days?"

She shrugged.

"Any family?"

"An aunt, an uncle, and a cousin. And to save you the trouble of asking, since it always follows, my mom took off when I was barely out of diapers, and I don't know where my dad is, much less who he is." She hoped he didn't hear the tremor of bitterness in words she tried to deliver in a bored monotone. But given the fact that Nate now gaped at her, again ignoring his sandwich, he must have.

He collected himself. "That must have been hard, growing up without parents. My mom died when I was just a kid, and my dad remarried five years ago." His jaw tensed, and he set down his sandwich and took a drink of soda before returning his attention to Carly. "You said you worked at the *Gazette*. What do you do now?"

"I'm between jobs."

"Funny, so am I."

"I got fired." She might as well be honest.

He grinned. "Me, too."

Her eyes opened wider. "You're kidding?"

"Dead serious."

"Wow, talk about odd—us being in the same boat. I'm not sure it's something I want to talk about, but I have to admit it's good being in like company."

"Same here." His smile switched to full-blown and knocked Carly a little off kilter. The guy was attractive, likeable, and nice, but, she reminded herself, she didn't want a relationship.

"As for what I'm doing now, I'm gathering information to write a guidebook for beginners, by me—a beginner—of what to expect on the Long Trail."

"I wondered what that mini recorder was for; I figured you were recording things for a personal journal. A lot of hikers do that sort of thing."

"Nope, I'm formulating a guidebook. I know there's a market, but I'm hoping my inexperience as a hiker won't cause problems in selling the idea. I doubt my old boss would give me the time of day as far as references go after the chewing out I got from him—long story; I don't want to go there. But I have other connections in the publishing industry and the media, so we'll see."

This time, she couldn't mistake his reaction. Nate became withdrawn, almost detached. He polished off the rest of his sandwich and his side of red potatoes in silence, and Carly concentrated on her meal, too. The stuffed mushrooms were zesty with garlic, just the way she liked them, and the soup was rich and smooth, perfect to take away the chill in her body. Too bad the warmth didn't reenter their conversation.

Nate wiped his mouth. "I should call it a night. I'm beat, and we need to get an early start tomorrow."

"Sure." Carly floundered, a bit disconcerted by his abrupt behavior. "If you're still feeling bushed tomorrow, I always have an extra protein shake."

The answering chuckle he gave was weak, and as she went to her room to take care of her laundry, she scolded herself. So what if he didn't want to spend the rest of the evening talking with her? That was what she wanted—her own space and no unwelcome advances. He seemed to have received her oft-repeated message loud and clear. So since everything now pointed in her favor, it made no sense that Carly should feel upset that he'd done exactly as she'd asked him.

⁂

The next day, the trail grew narrow, the overgrowth looming high along the sides, the path shooting up then down with what seemed neither rhyme nor reason. At lunch, they stopped at one of the shelters and met some AT hikers, those hiking the Appalachian Trail. Since both it and the Long Trail traveled the same path for one hundred miles, Nate was surprised these were the first AT hikers they'd met. The robust, middle-aged married couple were hiking the trail for their twenty-fifth anniversary, and Nate admired their courage in tackling it.

Carly seemed distant, which for once made Nate glad. The trail lay cluttered with countless rocks and massive tree roots, requiring every bit of attention.

Last night, when she had confessed she was a reporter, warning bells had gone off inside Nate, and the tragedy of his family's dilemma attacked him full force. He didn't appreciate the unwanted reminder, though he realized Carly wasn't to blame. She couldn't have known his story. No one did except Ted and Jill, whom he'd sworn to secrecy. And Nate planned to keep it that way.

He was sure Carly's journalistic blood would simmer to a boil if she knew that one of the most sought-after and evasive sources of recent headline news to hit southern Vermont hiked a few feet behind her. No longer would she avoid him; he would be running from her. Remembering his narrow escapes from the media, his "running" might become reality. And he couldn't let that happen.

He needed this hike. He had started to feel a closeness to God he hadn't experienced in months. For some reason, his town had marked his entire family as outcasts for one man's sins. Nate would never understand that, but he'd felt the full brunt of their bitter rejection. Here with Ted's church group, Nate enjoyed acceptance and anonymity; he didn't want to lose that.

When they reached the shelter where they would spend the night, a group of hikers who'd arrived before them invited their group to share in a weenie roast. While Carly didn't eat their food, she did participate in the light conversation as they all gathered around the fire and compared experiences they'd had while on the trail. She sat across from Nate, and he found his gaze wandering to her often. When she would suddenly look at him, he would shift his attention to something else like a misbehaving kid.

Kim excused herself, and soon after that, Carly left, too. Nate hesitated when she headed away from the shelter. Should he follow or just trust that she wouldn't wander too far in the dark and would know to stay out of trouble?

The answer, from previous experience, made him quietly groan, and he excused himself and set off in the direction she'd taken. He moved around the shelter and almost jumped out of his skin as he came close to mowing down both Carly and Kim.

Both girls squealed in shock, and Kim beamed her flashlight into Nate's face.

"Looking for someone?" Carly asked, her brow lifted, her tone steady.

As he worked to regain his bearings, Nate blocked the light from his eyes with his hand. He gave a disgusted chuckle and shook his head. "You would think I'd know better by now. Could you please shine that thing somewhere else?"

"Hey," Carly's tone came softer, "I was just teasing."

Kim lowered the light, and it flickered. "Rats. Looks like I need new batteries. Me and Carly were just about to play cards.

We could make it a game of Hearts if you want to join us."

About to refuse, Nate noticed Carly's expression, what he could see of it. Was the twilight playing tricks with his mind, or did she actually look hopeful that he might agree? He thought it over; a game of cards wasn't a journalistic interview, and he needed to unwind.

"Maybe just one game."

"Great," Kim enthused. "I have a candle, too. I'll get it." She scampered off.

"A candle?" Nate arched his brow.

Carly laughed. "Well, we can't exactly play by the light of the moon since there isn't one tonight."

"Good point." They walked to the front of the shelter.

Kim met them with a lit candle, using her hand to shield the flame.

"Why do you think the front is fenced in like a half gate?" Kim asked about the shelter as Nate opened the gate for her and Carly.

Nate didn't want to speculate, but he knew about recent bear sightings, and in the winter, porcupines made a nuisance of themselves. "Probably to keep out the animals."

"But animals are everywhere," Kim insisted. "It just seems sort of weird, is all."

Two campers not from their group lay sound asleep, huddled in a far corner. Kim dribbled wax on an old boxlike crate to secure the candle. Carly dealt them each a hand. Even with the flickering light, it wasn't easy to see the larger-than-usual numbers or colors of the cards, but Nate didn't care. The two girls were chatterbugs when together, though they spoke in quiet murmurs so as not to awaken the other hikers. Nate enjoyed hearing more of Carly's past when Kim asked her specific questions. From the little he remembered, Goosebury was a nice town. At least some small towns were nice.

Realizing the direction his thoughts had twisted, Nate pushed them to a back corner of his brain and concentrated on the good company. The lazy buzz of cicadas filled the night, and Kim rubbed her eyelids behind her glasses and yawned. "Well, that's it for me. My eyes hurt, and I'm beat—though not at cards." She laughed.

"That's right, rub it in," Carly joked.

"I'll walk you to your tent." The fence around the shelter bothered Nate more than he cared to let Kim and Carly know.

"You don't have to."

But Nate had already risen to his feet. Carly also stood.

"We have another long day ahead of us tomorrow. I think I'll call it quits as well."

Because Kim's tent was closest, they dropped her off first.

"Keep the candle." She handed it to Carly. "You can give it back tomorrow. It's creepy without a moon. Dangerous, too."

Wishing his slim flashlight wasn't behind in his backpack, Nate walked with Carly to the tent she'd pitched farther down the line. They seemed to have run out of things to talk about, and Nate wondered if Carly also felt an odd stirring in the air, a sense of awkward anticipation. He shot her a sidelong glance.

She held the candle at shoulder level. The flame illumined her already exotic features, giving her an almost otherworldly glow. Nate held his breath at her beauty. All she needed was a beaded dress and studded headband to look the part of a real Native American princess.

She turned to face him as they reached her tent. Nate detected her uneasiness as she finally lifted the gaze of her huge, dark eyes to his. He could get lost in those eyes and not mind it one bit.

"Nate, I know we didn't hit it off from the beginning, again my fault. But during this week of getting to know you, I've come to realize I do want your friendship. I can't help but feel, what with the way you've been acting today, that I did something or said something to upset you at the inn. So, if I did, I'm sorry, and I'd like to be trail mates again."

"Meaning no more veiled thoughts of pushing me into a creek?"

She grinned. "As long as you don't hoist me up and dump me in it first."

Nate couldn't help but return her soft smile. "Carly." He laid his fingers against the sleeve on her upper arm in a manner meant to reassure. "Just so you know, my behavior today had nothing to do with anything you've done. I've been going through some hard times, and last night brought it all back."

Carly gave a nod. "I can understand that." She moved the candle between them, her fingers almost touching his chest. "Any time you want to unload, I make a decent listener."

"I'll remember that." His words came quietly, his mind spinning to another track. Standing so close to her, he felt connected. Her eyes drew him; her lips parted. If not for the chance of scorching his chin with the flame from her candle, he would have leaned forward to kiss her. Even more shocking, she looked as if she wanted him to.

He gave a slight shake of his head and retreated a step. "Well, I need to call it a night. Dawn will be here before you know it. So, uh. . .yeah, good night."

"Do you need the candle?" Carly called after him.

"No, I can make it."

Seconds later in the pitch dark, he stumbled over a tree root and fell flat on his hands and knees.

"You okay?"

At the worry in Carly's voice, he hurried to his feet and brushed off his jeans. "Sure. I meant to do that."

She giggled at his silly response, and Nate's heart gave a light jump at the unexpected sound of her velvety laughter, but he continued his trek toward his tent. He wasn't about to return to collect any candle, because this time he would give in and kiss her. And Nate had no idea how to handle this sudden, mind-boggling switch from thinly veiled hostility to open friendship. He'd wanted her friendship, sure, but nothing else. And as far as he knew, the powers that be hadn't written a guidebook on the best defense against falling for another person.

Falling for another person. . .the thought almost made him trip again. No way was he falling for Carly. No way. . .

He readied for bed that night with more force than necessary, unzipping his sleeping bag so fast he felt grateful he hadn't knocked the zipper off the metal teeth. Nate had come on this hike to get away from complications and to get in tune with God. Though the latter had brought results, the former still needed improvements.

He had no desire to start a romantic relationship.

seven

Over the next few days, the hike turned rougher, the trail steeper, filled with copious natural stone steps, many of them uphill. But where there was uphill, downhill must follow, and Carly wondered when the trail would level off, if ever. At times she had to use her hands to climb exposed ledges. Still, despite the strenuous workouts, the blisters she nursed, frequent rain, and thick black flies and other insects near all bodies of water, she was glad she'd come. The alpine region through which they trekked made her grateful for the warm clothes she'd packed, and the brisk, clean air brought new life to her lungs. The awesome views at the summits of each mountain were masterpieces to her eyes, and she took so many pictures, she was glad she'd invested in a second camera card. The sensation of being secluded safely away in nature's quiet corner helped Carly to relax and forget about the real world for a while.

She and Nate had become true "trail mates," and she found it curious he hadn't been nearly as talkative with her today as in recent days. A slight tension sizzled between them, though his attitude toward her remained friendly and helpful.

Their lives had produced a pattern. During the days, they hiked, climbed, and sometimes fell or otherwise banged themselves up. During the evenings, they relaxed, ate, and got to know one another better. Carly had also become good friends with Kim, amazed at how intelligent the girl was. She talked about the regular things all teenage girls enjoy— favorites in music, fads, and boys—but at times when they played cards, their conversation took a deeper route, and Carly got a good look inside the girl's mind. For herself, she hadn't shared much beyond the basics of her personal life, and she intended to keep it that way. She never mentioned Jake's name; just thinking about him put a sour taste in her mouth.

"Carly."

The presence of Nate coming up behind her so abruptly and murmuring her name threw her, and she startled.

"Hold still. Don't move."

The words themselves brought all manner of terrible visions to mind. "What is it?"

"Just hold still." Nate's hand made a quick swipe through her hair, and she did all she could not to scream.

"A bug? There was a bug in my hair?" The inchworms falling from the trees the other day had been bad enough to try to avoid.

"A spider."

Just the name gave her shivers. She and the eight-legged creatures didn't get along well—she always gave them their distance. Regardless that she knew the vicious invader was gone, she swept her fingers through her hair.

"It was pretty small. About the size of a nickel, with legs."

"You are not helping any." She gave up combing her fingers through her hair and bent double, flipping her hair over to whisk her fingers through as if washing it.

"I did get it out."

"I know, but it might have had babies."

"In your hair?" She heard the amusement in his voice.

"They carry them in a sac, you know. My aunt stepped on one once—hundreds of tiny babies went scurrying all over the floor." Just saying it gave her another dose of shivers.

"Well, no worries. I see no more creatures running through your hair. Tiny or otherwise."

"Thanks." The word came out droll.

"So, I take it you don't like spiders?" Nate had the audacity to grin, and Carly could have cheerfully pushed him down the rock step they'd just climbed.

"Name one person who does," she shot back.

"Spiderman."

His crazy answer made her roll her eyes. "Those people not belonging to the fictional world of Marvel comics."

"I'm impressed. You know your comic books."

"Not really. My cousin grew up on them."

"Any sisters, brothers? I hardly know anything about you."

"I'm an only child. And anyway, you know all that's important to know, and more besides." Carly shrugged, uneasy with the turn of conversation and her memory of spouting off about her parents. "Whereas I know next to nothing about you. How come?"

Nate looked ahead on the path. "We should catch up to the others."

"Well, that was an evasive answer if ever I heard one."

"Not much to tell." He didn't meet her eyes, instead showing extreme interest in their surroundings. "But I guess we could resume this conversation at lunch if you want."

"I'll hold you to that."

And she did.

As they gathered at Birch Glen Camp, Carly put aside her noonday habit of reciting notes into her mini recorder and, hands clasping her thighs, she sank to her knees in front of Nate.

"I'm all ears," she said, her manner pure innocence.

"What?"

"For the story of your life."

He groaned. "You have a good memory."

"I have a great memory. So how about it?"

Nate took a long swig from his water bottle and capped it. "Well, to begin with, I was born."

Carly's brows arched. "Why does this sound strangely like an intro to *David Copperfield?*"

Nate laughed. "I'm surprised you recognized it."

"I'm a writer, Nate. I have an interest in books. But I'm surprised you brought up a classic. Somehow you don't strike me as being a literary bug."

"You're right; I'm not. Old memories still lodged in there from high school, I guess. I had to write a report on that book. I almost sweat drops of blood over that paper."

Carly laughed. "Ah. That explains it. So, I know you were born, and that your name is not David Copperfield. What about your family?"

Did she imagine it, or did Nate tense?

"A father, a married sister, stepmother, stepbrother. Like I said before, Mom died when I was a kid, and Dad remarried several years ago." He shrugged. "Not much to tell."

"You're too modest; I'll bet there are a lot of interesting things about you." A flash of heat swept over Carly, and she noted his surprised look at her telltale words. "I mean, everyone has stories of interest. So let me help you along a little. What did you do before you got fired?"

"You're a curious sort, aren't you? Is this an interview?"

"No, strictly off the record. I guess you could say curiosity runs deep in my blood." She shrugged as if that explained it. "Besides, I told you my former job title, so it seems only fair you should reciprocate. Isn't that what buddies do—swap jokes and trade woes?"

"Oh, so *now* you want to be my buddy," Nate said in mock amusement. "Now that the spotlight is trained on me."

She gave a sweet, not-so-innocent smile, and he snorted.

"Okay, *buddy*, I was a tour guide for a small organization in southern Vermont. I basically carted people around the countryside to places of interest."

"And you don't call that interesting?" Carly could see Nate as a tour guide; he had that friendly quality with people, even strangers. And he was careful to watch out for others getting off on the wrong trail—literally. Carly remembered when he'd stopped Kim from using a side trail. She hadn't seen the blue blaze marking the tree. Maybe that's where he'd gotten his protective nature, from his job. Or maybe it was just a part of who he was.

"What?"

She made an effort to stop grinning. "Just thinking you would have made a great tour guide, is all."

"A compliment, coming from you?" He gathered his brows in pretend amazement. "I think someone must have slipped something into your mud-protein shake."

She laughed. "Okay, okay. I know I was pretty hard on you at first, but maybe I was wrong about you. Give a girl a break."

Hearing footsteps, Carly swung her head around. "Hey, Kimmers."

The teen waved back, but Carly noted her face seemed tense as she walked on into the shelter and sat down at a table there. Maybe she'd had words with her dad; Carly had spotted them in intense conversation earlier that morning.

"Do you give everyone nicknames?" Nate asked. "I've heard you call Jill Ju-Ju, and Sierra, Cat."

"Only my friends. Jill got dubbed Ju-Ju because of her desire to always fix things. Like Zu-Zu's petals." She looked at him when he only stared. "From the Capra movie *It's a Wonderful Life*."

"Oh, right."

"And Cat, well, with her pretty auburn hair and green eyes, she just looks catlike. Kim became Kimmers because the word reminded me of glimmers and shimmers; she's always so bubbly." Carly tilted her head and stared at Nate in deep reflection. "I guess since we're trail mates now, I need to think up a name for you, too. *Trail Mate* just doesn't cut it." She grinned wickedly. "Maybe Alfalfa. . .Kelpie. Or Shadow would work. Creek Scourge or Brook Rogue are options, too."

"Cute." Nate reached over to tug a hank of her hair, as if they were children.

"Hey—only kidding!" She laughed. "And no one touches my hair."

"Right, I'll remember that for the future."

"You'd better," she said in a menacing tone.

"Does that order count in the case of any future arachnid dwellers?" His grin teased. "Or do I have permission then?"

She couldn't help it; she swatted his arm.

"Hey!" Nate pulled back, laughing.

"Hi, you two." Sierra walked up to them. "Ted wants everyone to gather for a short reading. Since Jill's sick, we're camping here, and we won't be having discussion tonight."

"Ju-Ju's sick?" Alarm wiped the smile from Carly's mouth. She hoped her friend hadn't gotten hold of some bad water.

"Yeah, probably a twenty-four-hour virus. With all this rain we've had to hike in, it's a wonder all of us aren't sick."

True, but rain only augmented an illness; it didn't start one. And they'd been wearing protective rain gear.

"Ted said this might set us back a day. We won't know if she can manage the hike until tomorrow morning."

Carly shrugged off her worries for Jill and stood to her feet. The only part of this group hike that made her uncomfortable had been the devotional readings with discussion following. Most nights during the onset of the hike, she'd sought escape in her tent, but not wanting to be rude to her hosts, she had joined the group on other occasions.

She felt like an interloper during those times Ted or another person read Bible passages aloud, followed by conversation, sometimes intense, as each gave their views. She didn't believe in any of what they said, had never been raised to accept it, so she couldn't take part and sat silent, a reluctant observer. But at some point, something infinitesimal had metamorphosed within her in such a quiet way she'd hardly noticed when her feelings had begun to change.

Before this hike, she had doubted the existence of God and argued such a viewpoint to the ground when anyone brought it up. Being so attuned with nature and absent from the continual distractions of town life and the electronic devices that were part of her existence had quieted her mind and made her think. Here, she experienced a different world; maybe not a better world than the one she knew in Goosebury, but one that offered mental peace and emotional solitude, as well as physical challenge. A world where she could stand on summits so elevated that if she reached up, she could touch the sky and then look over the panoramic landscape far below and all around her. A world clustered amid trees and rocks and water, riddled with snow-peaked mountains and hidden valleys. A world where it became more and more difficult to accept her belief that life had come into being by chance.

As Ted read aloud, Carly watched a shaft of afternoon sunlight stream through the branches of nearby trees. A flash of orange streaked through the light, and she saw a fire salamander dart over the ground from under a log and race through the tall grass.

How could this all have just happened? She'd never really thought about it, just went along with her family's ideas; but the detail in each leaf, each flower, each creature, diverse and beautiful in its own way, had to have been crafted by a master hand.

Shivers went through her as her mind began to open up to the concept she had always denied.

There is a God.

From what she'd witnessed of her friends Leslie and Jill and seen of their lives, she was ninety-nine percent certain this all-Supreme Being was the God of the Bible. The God who had made a heaven and a hell. And knowing that, Carly experienced a stirring of personal doubt, guilt—and fear.

If they were right and Carly was wrong, then she was in even worse trouble than she'd thought.

❧

The next day, Nate questioned his decision to ask Carly if she wanted to tag along for a short, four-mile spur down a side trail, but the words shot out of his mouth before he could reel them back.

"Sure." She looked at him, curious. "I'll get my backpack."

Nate didn't blame her for her surprise. One minute, he retreated from her; the next minute, he invited her company. At breakfast, he'd barely talked to her. But he didn't want to make the trek alone for more than just safety's sake.

"How's Jill doing?" he asked when Carly returned. "I saw you go to her tent earlier."

Carly finished buckling the strap around her. "She's a trooper, though I know she hates to hold everyone back like this. But she hasn't been able to keep anything down and is too exhausted to move. Sounds like that virus that was going around Goosebury before we took off."

"She shouldn't feel bad about holding anyone back. This is a much-needed diversion. Ted has been running everyone too hard, trying to get so many miles in each day. It's nice to kick back for a while and rest. Especially before tackling the Camel's Hump. That mountain has challenged the best of hikers."

"And we're going on a short hike to relax?" Carly grinned.

"Okay, well it's nice for the others who are new to this sort of thing. Me, I can't sit still for long. If I do, my muscles may atrophy."

"Same here." Carly cast a glance up and sobered. "But the sky looks like rain."

"So when have we ever let a little moisture stop us?"

She laughed again. "Agreed. Should we invite the others?"

"I did. They'd rather rest, and Ted is busy taking care of Jill."

They'd only traveled about a mile before the rain hit. Nate pulled up the hood of his rain gear, and Carly did the same with hers. Instead of the mild shower he'd hoped for, the precipitation became a deluge, hindering their ability to walk.

Carly grabbed his arm and pointed off the trail to an area where the trees formed a canopy. "We could stay there until this passes."

"Under the trees? I don't think that's a good idea."

"There's no lightning, and even if there were, on a mountain-side covered with so many trees, the chance of a strike are about one in a million."

She took off without waiting for him to answer. "Lady, do you always flirt with danger?" he called after her.

Shaking his head, Nate had no choice but to follow. The other option that flitted through his brain—dragging her back to camp—didn't seem a wise choice.

Once under the thick, sheltering boughs, which let in scant droplets of rain, Nate had to admit it was nice not to have to clear his vision by continually wiping water out of his eyes. With a little smile, Carly tipped her head back against the trunk, her eyelids sweeping down as if to absorb her surroundings and the few drops that landed on her skin.

Nate took the liberty of studying her face. Her lashes wet, they still had a curl at their tips, thick and lush, as natural as the gentle arch of her eyebrows. In this wilderness hike, the women didn't bother with makeup, and Nate knew all he saw of Carly was natural. Rain only accentuated her beauty as the clear beaded drops played with the light, emphasizing her high cheekbones, the gentle slope of her forehead, the smooth line of her nose, which ended in a soft rounded tip. Underneath, her lips were full and moist.

A strange sensation knotted his throat, almost painful, as he stared at her mouth, then back up to her closed eyes.

"You're staring at me," she said. "Stop it."

Surprised she realized it, he felt a bit disconcerted. "So, what, now you have radar in your eyelids?"

At that, her lips curled into an amused smile. "All women do, didn't you know?" She opened her eyes, and Nate wondered if it was his recent scrutiny of her features that made him notice how shimmering dark they were and how big. "It's the only way we can keep ourselves armed against unwanted attention."

"Right." Nate looked back out at the trees. What was he doing? What was he thinking? Of course, Carly didn't want anything to do with him on a more serious level; he also had no desire to take it further. They were trail mates on the path to friendship. Nothing more.

For the remainder of the downpour, Nate focused on the range of trees surrounding them and their diversity of textures. Thick hardwoods and slender pines stood with one another, opposites in traits but equals in their cause for existence. Each trunk maintained its own space, not allowing the other trees inside its circle, but still, they all somehow managed to work together in harmony to give the mountainside beauty, the animals shelter and food.

"Nate, listen." Carly looked toward the west. "Do you hear that?"

Broken from his wry musings, he struggled to listen. The rain had lessened, and he could hear what sounded like a faint bawling, almost a bleating.

"Whatever it is sounds as if it's in trouble." Carly moved toward the sound.

"Carly, I wouldn't do that."

Regardless, she continued her course.

"Woman, don't you ever listen to anyone?" he muttered in frustration, following her.

She stopped at the edge of some overgrowth, pulling it back. Even above the sounds of trickling water, he heard her gasp. "Nate! Come look."

He joined her, looking over her shoulder. A cream-spotted fawn nestled on the grasses, its head low. Its frail body was no more than the size of a large housecat, and its soft, pointed ears lay to the side as its huge black eyes watched them.

"Oh, Nate. Isn't she the most adorable thing you've ever seen?" Carly's voice became soft, wondering. "And the poor baby's shivering. Do you think she's cold or scared?"

Nate watched Carly lean forward as though she might pet it.

"Carly—don't." He grabbed her arm, this time not allowing her the choice of going against him. "I know it's cute and it's tempting to pet, but you shouldn't touch any wild animal, especially a baby." Releasing his hold on her, he studied the fawn, whose bleats had grown more frantic. "It looks like it's only a few weeks old."

"Where's the mother?" Carly scanned the area as if hoping to spot a doe, then turned back to the fawn. "You don't think the poor thing has been abandoned, do you?"

"No, that's how a doe treats its young. It hides them somewhere safe and returns when the fawns need to feed."

"But what if she doesn't come back? What if this poor little girl is left all alone without her mother to take care of her? Look at her now. She's so fragile, so vulnerable. She looks as if a strong gust of wind might blow her away. What if a bear finds her?"

"The pelt helps to camouflage the fawn against would-be predators." Nate watched doubt and compassion play across Carly's face, noting how she'd instantly labeled the fawn a female and not a male.

Carly swung her head around to pinpoint him with flashing eyes. "We can't leave her here all alone!"

"There's nothing else we can do, Carly. We can't take it back with us. We need to respect the wildlife. And hard as it may seem when things look bad, we can't tamper with nature's order, much less violate state laws that forbid anyone other than a wildlife rehabilitator from intervening with sick animals."

"That just seems so wrong," she fumed. "So let me get this straight, according to the system, we let a helpless creature, no more than a few weeks old, die because man's law says we must. That's just not right." Tears shone in her eyes, astonishing Nate. "Under extenuating circumstances, I think some laws need to be vetoed or rewritten."

"This is more than just about the fawn, isn't it?" he asked softly.

He watched her lips part in surprise, watched her clamp her teeth and her jaw grow firm as a hard glint shone in her eyes while she struggled to maintain composure. Struggled, and lost. To his bafflement, she bowed her head, and her shoulders shook. He'd never seen Carly so vulnerable, like the baby fawn.

Compassion urged him to move forward and take her in his arms, while common sense warned him to back away while he still could. His heart triumphed in the battle with his mind, and compassion won.

He pulled her close, and she stiffened as his hands gently pressed against her back. "It's okay, Carly. It's okay."

She relaxed against him, little by little, dropping her forehead to his collarbone. Along with his sympathy for whatever brought on her mute sobs, Nate couldn't help but realize he enjoyed the soft feel of her in his arms. As she released quiet tears mixed with the gentle sprinkle of rain, Nate smoothed a hand along her slick hair. Her hood had fallen away at some point, and just as he thought about plucking it up and replacing it, she lifted her eyes to look at him. Glazed with tears, they'd never appeared so beautiful, so soft. Her lashes curled in gentle spikes, her lips trembled.

"I'm sorry, I—"

"Shh." With a slight shake of his head, Nate moved his hands to cradle her jaw, then leaned in to kiss her.

Her lips were cool, soft, wet from the rain, and what Nate had told himself he intended to be a token of gentle reassurance turned into much more. He brushed his lips over hers and heard her gasp. He couldn't remember when he'd last felt like this, or why he'd been avoiding it. Stunned, he pulled away a fraction and looked into her slightly unfocused, night-dark eyes.

"What are you doing?" She breathed a little faster, her features soft, uncertain, her lips that he'd just touched with his parted and trembling.

"I don't know, but if you figure it out, don't tell me," he whispered before leaning in to kiss her again. To his shock, Carly whimpered and pressed against him, sliding her hands up around his neck as their kiss altered into one of mutual need. He moved his hands to her back and responded with equal fervor, until suddenly she pressed her hands against his chest and broke their kiss, pushing away. He released her.

She retreated a few steps, wouldn't meet his eyes. Nate stood motionless and couldn't keep from staring at her.

"I shouldn't have done that," he said after a taut silence elapsed.

"I shouldn't have responded."

"But you did, and I did." Nate's voice was low. "So where

does that leave us, Carly?"

She shook her head in frustration. "Don't ask; I don't know. Maybe we should just call it a mistake."

"A mistake is something never meant to happen. Neither of us may have expected this just now, but I think if we're honest with each other, we've both felt the currents all along."

Carly shut her eyes, and her lips parted, revealing to Nate he'd been correct. "I don't want a relationship, Nate. Not now. I just came out of a really bad one."

He didn't want a relationship, either, so why was he pushing her? He shoved his hands in his pockets. Another minute passed before he spoke.

"Mind telling me what that was all about earlier?"

"You mean my crying jag?" The cynicism crept back into her voice. "I thought you would have figured it out after what I told you at the restaurant. My mom abandoned me on my aunt's doorstep when I was a kid, remember?" She shrugged as if it didn't matter. "Call it a sudden weakness that overcame me when I saw the fawn. I'm really over those days, and I have no idea why I carried on so."

Nate doubted she was as emotionally invincible as she wanted him to believe. "Carly, it really is okay to cry."

Her brow arched wryly. "Are you speaking from experience or just saying what feels right at the moment?"

"Both."

She didn't answer. After a moment, she looked away from him and to the fronds that covered the baby deer. "What about her?"

He knew he would regret the words that formed in his mind, but they escaped regardless. "I guess we could stick around for a while, out of sight, and wait to see that the mama comes back. With the way the fawn was bawling, if the doe is nearby, she'll be coming soon."

Carly's smile brightened the day, making him glad he'd suggested it.

"Thank you, Nate."

Together, they moved away from the fawn and among the trees closer to the trail, hidden from view of the fawn's bed but still within range to spy. Nate wondered how long they would have to stand there until Carly's hopes were satisfied; he didn't want to wait for hours. Worse, he had no guarantee the mother would return. The doe might have been hurt or killed by a carnivore. Yet Nate had a feeling Carly wouldn't budge from her observation post until the doe made an appearance.

As the minutes passed, he thought of a multitude of questions he wanted to ask but reasoned it better to leave such things unspoken at this point. Normally, he enjoyed the sounds of nature and didn't always like to talk, but their earlier words felt as if they'd been left teetering on a precipice, undone and unfinished. His only worry was that if he said too much, he would push her over, along with the conversation.

"Nate, it's okay. Really."

"What?" Startled she had spoken, he looked at her.

"You're wondering what to say to me about my mother. Or maybe you're wondering if you should bring up our kiss. So let me save you the trouble; I'd rather not talk about either."

"You know, Carly, it baffles me how you always think you can read my mind."

She offered him one swift glance at his somber words. "So, was I wrong?"

Nate didn't want to admit that this time she was dead on target. But the thought of continued silence oppressed him. He fished about in his mind for the right words, but those that came to him seemed too trite. Those he longed to speak, too personal. What did someone say to a woman like Carly in a situation like this?

"Nate." Her excited whisper broke through his frustrated musings. "Look."

At the edge of the trees where he had kissed her, a doe moved with wary grace, then stopped and sniffed the ground. He hoped the delicate creature wouldn't be able to discern their scent, that the rain had washed it away. If the doe didn't return to the fawn, Nate wasn't sure what Carly would do.

As they watched, the doe lifted her head, alert. The fawn bawled louder as if sensing its mama nearby. After another tense wait, the doe moved to the tall fronds where she'd hidden the fawn.

"A happy ending," Carly breathed with a wistful smile. "That was worth every second of standing in the rain to see." She looked at him. "Again, thank you."

He smiled and nodded. "Are you ready to return to camp?"

"You don't want to continue the hike?"

"The others might get worried if we're gone too long and send out a search party." Nate was only half-joking. "Ted's pretty upset about Jill, and I don't want to add to his troubles by not showing up for lunch."

"I've been worried about her, too," she said as they started the hike back.

"Well, it's like I told Ted, she has nothing that a good amount of loving, prayer, and rest won't cure."

Carly didn't respond, and Nate wondered which of the three she didn't agree with. He doubted it was the second, since she was with a church group, and didn't think it could be the last. Everyone complained at one time or another that Ted pushed them too hard. So that left loving, and considering the glimpse she'd given him into her past and the knowledge that she'd just come out of a bad relationship, Nate had a sneaking suspicion Carly had rarely been on the receiving end of any real affection.

The sudden thought that he might be the one to change

all that sent an unexpected rush of adrenaline through his veins. One minute he fought the idea of a relationship with her; the next, he welcomed it. She was fire and water, ice and wind—her passionate nature, her free spirit attracting him like no other woman had done. He had enjoyed the times they'd conversed on friendly levels, and a part of him had been drawn like a moth to her flame when they'd exchanged heated banter. She confused him, exasperated him, magnetized him, and fascinated him.

He was beginning to feel as mixed up as Carly acted.

eight

That night as the others gathered around the campfire, Carly held back. She couldn't explain why on other occasions she hadn't minded joining the group devotions so much, even if she did feel as if she was on the outside looking in, but tonight she not only felt like an outsider but also a hypocrite.

Her mind still whirled with her earlier conversation with Nate, not to mention his kiss, which she'd been shocked to find herself not only accepting but returning, and she didn't feel as if she could paste a smile on her face one more night and pretend something she didn't feel.

She tended to her needs, hoping Kim might still be up and would want to talk. The teenager had left the group earlier, complaining her eyes hurt.

Carly poked her head in the shelter, where Kim and her father had opted to stay because of all the rain, but even in the dark, she could see that Kim's sleeping bag lay flat. Confused, Carly looked back toward the latrine. She had just come from there and would have passed Kim on her return, but she checked again anyway. It, too, was empty.

Before she created a panic, Carly walked around the shelter on the outskirts of the trees, searching for Kim. The increasing darkness made it difficult to see, even with the light from the fire ring that three other campers huddled around.

She glanced toward the small group in front of Ted's tent. Jill sat by his side, and Carly was relieved to see her friend must be feeling better. The moon washed the circle of hikers in its glow, and someone had placed a camp lantern in the middle, providing more light. A sweeping glance in their direction was enough to tell her that Kim hadn't rejoined the group.

She hurried toward them, and they all turned to look.

"Kim's missing."

"What?" Her father, Frank, tensed, then shot to his feet. "What do you mean 'missing'?"

"She's not in her bedroll or anywhere else. I checked."

"That's not possible—she knows better than to go off by herself." Even as he said the words, Frank grabbed the lantern from the middle of the ring.

"Maybe she's just hanging around at the back of the shelter," Sierra suggested.

"Why would she do that?" Frank insisted.

Sierra shrugged. "Just an idea."

"She's not there; I looked already," Carly inserted.

They all gaped at one another, then moved into action. A quick search of the immediate grounds and a short inter-rogation of the other campers brought no success. Clouds now covered the moon, dimming what little light it gave. Frank looked about ready to come apart, and Jill took his hand. "First, we pray. Then, we search."

A little disconcerted, Carly didn't pull away when Sierra took one of her hands and Nate the other as they formed a circle. She looked around at everyone's bowed heads, then dropped her head as well, though she kept her eyes open, peering at their faces in the faint firelight.

"Lord, we ask You to keep Kim safe and help us find her. We trust You to watch over our young friend and give us wisdom in this situation. In Jesus's name, amen."

"Amen," the group echoed, and Carly whispered her own amen, feeling she should say something, too. She wasn't sure what to believe anymore. But that these people, all of them intelligent and normal, did rely on a higher power and first turned to God in their time of crisis shook her, made her think. She may not understand the source that propelled their actions, but she respected the sincerity she witnessed in their expressions. They believed what they preached; not only that, they lived it.

"We split up with our buddies, each of us taking a different route," Ted said. "No one goes alone. Frank, you come with me." He clapped a hand to his shoulder in silent support.

The three hikers not of their group came up to them. "We overheard you talking, and we'd like to help."

"Thanks," Ted said. "We can use every pair of eyes we can get. If you'll backtrack up the main path and search there?"

"Sure."

The three men left, armed with their backpacks and flashlights. Ted assigned the rest of the group areas in which to search.

"Be sure and take your backpacks. You never know when you'll need them."

Frank's expression grew grim. "Kim doesn't have hers." He shone his light on the dark blue canvas painted with pink neon hearts.

A pall of silence descended before Jill spoke. "We'll find her, Frank."

"Are you sure you shouldn't stay behind, love?" Ted said. "With the camp emptying out, if Kim does return, someone should stay here to tell her what's up."

"What happened to 'every pair of eyes we can get'?" Jill's words were light and serious at the same time. "I'm better, not so crook. Kim's gone walkabout, and I want to search, too."

Jill might not feel so sick, but her face was still too pale, and she'd hardly touched her dinner. Jill was stubborn when it came to certain ideas like wanting to fix things for others, so Carly treaded with caution, deciding it best not to focus on her friend's sickness, but only on Kim. "Ted has a point, Ju-Ju. Kim might get scared if she comes back and no one's here. She might try and look for us. If someone stays behind, that won't happen."

Carly looked up to see Nate watch her with approval. That shocked her; she'd never had approval from any man. But it lifted her spirits, though she wasn't sure why she should care whether he approved of her or not.

Jill finally agreed, her reluctance obvious.

Ted eyed the group. "Whoever finds Kim, blow the whistle we gave you the first day. One, if all is okay. Two, if you need help." He said the last with a dismal sideways glance at Frank. "Don't worry about waking anyone since the other campers joined in the search, too."

"But they don't know about the whistle signals," Sierra said.

"I'll tell them; they're still within sight." Bart ran to catch up to the three.

Carly shrugged into her backpack and buckled it. Nate came up beside her. "You ready?"

She nodded, and together they walked to their assigned section in the east, combing the trees.

❧

Carly and Nate used their slim flashlights in a wide sweep and stayed no more than a few feet apart as they moved through undergrowth, pushing branches and bushes aside as they called Kim's name. In the distance, they heard the rustle and calls of the others and saw pinpoints of light to each side of them. Minutes ticked by, and Nate sensed Carly's fear heighten by her jerky movements. Despite his own worry for the teenager, he tried to reassure.

"Kim knows better than to go too far."

"She also knows better than to go anywhere alone without her trail mate," Carly shot back, concern lacing her voice.

"She's a bright kid. There must be a logical explanation for this."

Carly didn't respond.

"Any minute now, we'll hear a whistle blow or stumble across her ourselves." As dark as it was in these woods, the flashlights didn't help much.

"That's what I'm afraid of." Her words wavered.

"What?" He looked her way.

"I keep remembering that sign we ran across, about the two murdered hikers. What if someone's out there, and he's gotten hold of Kim?"

Nate took a moment to respond, since the same thought had flashed through his mind. "Hey." He reached out, slipping his arm around her shoulder, then pulled her into a one-armed hug. "None of that." Staring out at the black woods, he dropped a light kiss in her hair when she let her head drop to his shoulder. "I can't have my trail mate falling apart on me."

"You're right." She lifted her head, swiping at her eyes with her fingers. "This is getting us nowhere. It just hit me how very alone we are out here in this wilderness with no police to turn to, no emergency aid, no one really. Anything could happen."

"Carly, there's no use borrowing trouble. More than half of a person's worries never happen. We just have to trust God that this is all going to turn out for the best." The words seemed trite, but it was the best comfort he could offer.

He felt her stiffen against him. "I just don't get how you guys can believe that God is always there to make everything better."

You guys? Nate felt as if someone had punched him in the gut. "Carly, don't you believe in God?"

She pulled away. "We need to find Kim. We can talk about this later."

She was right, of course, and though Nate felt frustrated at their curtailed discussion, he moved along with Carly, putting all his efforts into finding the teenager.

They'd gone a short distance when suddenly Carly grabbed Nate's arm, stopping him. "Wait. Do you hear that?"

Nate held very still to listen. Amid the usual buzz and chirrup of insects, a faint warbling sounded in the distance.

"I think it's a bird or some kind of animal."

"Not that," Carly whispered. "That!" she exclaimed when the faint but distinct sound of someone crying came to them.

"It's coming from that direction." Nate pointed his flashlight. "Kim!"

Relief and anxiety mixed into one powerful surge. He hoped it was Kim and that she cried only because she was lost. They hurried as fast as they were able through the undergrowth.

"Kim!" Carly shouted, and Nate echoed her call.

"Over here!"

Grateful to hear the thin thread of Kim's voice, Nate changed direction toward a ten o'clock angle, increasing his pace and pushing away the shrubbery with a vengeance. Carly hurried behind him. Their flashlights picked up the teen at the same time. She sat cross-legged on the ground, her face stained with tears and clouded with relief, her glasses missing.

Carly rushed to her, hunkering down. "Kim, are you all right? What happened? Oh, my—look at your hands." In concern, she lifted the girl's palms from where they sat face up in her lap. Small red cuts crisscrossed the skin.

"I was trying to find my glasses," Kim said, her voice wobbly and hoarse. "I'm legally blind without them."

"Did you drop them here?" Carly searched the ground near her feet.

"I was running and fell. I swung my head around, and they flew off. My face was sweating—it's happened before when I swing around too fast."

With care, Carly looked through the brambles beside Kim while Nate pulled out his whistle and gave one extended blow.

The shrill noise shocked Kim into jerking her attention his way. "My dad's mad, isn't he?"

"Not so much mad as very worried," Nate assured. "What possessed you to take off like that, alone and off the path? You know the rule about trail mates, Kim."

Carly drew her hand back suddenly with a hiss, lifting her finger to her mouth to suck it.

"Be careful," Kim said. "There are thorns. That's partly how my hands got all scratched up."

"Let me help." Nate moved, careful to shine the flashlight on the ground to catch any possible reflection of the lenses. "Here, you hold the light," he said, handing Carly the flashlight, "and I'll look."

"I was doing okay," Carly muttered.

"Yeah, but my hands are tougher." He dug around through an area she hadn't yet explored. A thorn pierced the pad of his index finger. "Ow!" He pulled his hand away and shook it.

"Tougher, huh?"

He didn't miss her grin. "Just hold the light."

After pulling back a few brambles, he saw a blue earpiece sticking up at an angle. He plucked the glasses out, glad to see them in one piece.

"Here you go. They don't look damaged."

"Thanks." Kim took them from him, cleaning the lenses on her sweatshirt before slipping them over her ears. "It's good to be able to see again." Her words came dull.

"How did you get out here?" Carly asked.

Kim looked sheepish. "I took my gold watch off before I went to get water—I didn't want it getting wet and ruined, even though it is waterproof. It was my mom's," she finished sadly. "I don't wear it much, but today I did, and I had laid it on my backpack. But it must have fallen or something, because when I came back, some animal—I think it was a raccoon—found it and ran with it into the woods. So I chased it." She shrugged.

"In the dark?"

"It was still light then. I didn't know I'd get lost. When I realized the watch was really gone and the raccoon had gotten away, I didn't know where I was. I kept trying to find the path back, but instead I kept digging myself farther into the trees. I heard what sounded like a moose or maybe even a bear. It made an awful grunting noise. I got scared and ran, but I tripped over a tree root or something on the ground here, and my glasses flew off. By then it was dark."

Nate watched as Carly pulled a first-aid kit out of her backpack. "Hold the light while I take care of her hands," she addressed Nate.

This time, he obeyed as Carly washed the dirt and dried blood off Kim's palms with the water from her bottle, then swabbed them with antiseptic-soaked gauze from a foil packet.

"Feel like you can walk?" Nate asked.

"I think so." They helped her to her feet, giving her leverage underneath her arms. Kim hissed as she straightened her leg.

"You think it's sprained?" Carly asked.

"No, I've had those from playing softball. I think it's just scraped."

Still, Kim limped, and Nate slipped his arm around her waist to support her while she gripped his shoulder. It made for a slow trek back to camp, but the teen was already shaking so much, he didn't want to push their pace.

"My dad's going to be so mad," Kim said again, and Carly shared a look over Kim's head with Nate. He sensed her alarm and also wondered why Kim should be so worried about her father's reaction.

"I'm sure it'll all work out fine, Kimmers," Carly assured.

When they reached camp, Frank was already there, along with the others. As Kim nervously limped into the clearing, his face grew stern, his jaw clenched and unclenched, but tortured relief filled his eyes.

Nate let go of her, and Kim nervously adjusted her glasses and moved a few steps toward her father, awkward. "I'm sorry, Daddy."

Tension crackled through the air. "Kim," he said, emotion choking his words. "That was really stupid."

"I know."

He held out his arms to her, and she hurried into them. A flash of pain burned through Carly's heart, and she turned away, toward her tent. At times, she wished she had tried to find her own father. If she'd been sure of his identity, she might have attempted it. When she was little, she used to wonder if he even knew of her existence. According to her aunt, her mother had been wild, and she'd told Carly no one knew her father, least of all her mother. Not that her mother had been around much to ask. Still, Carly wondered. . .

"Carly?"

Nate's voice stopped her. She looked over her shoulder to where he still stood at the fringe of trees.

"If you're not sleepy, I'd like to talk."

Mentally, she felt wide-awake, though physically her muscles begged for rest. The search for Kim had given her a second wind, yet she didn't feel as if she could drag herself another step.

Against her better judgment, she nodded and followed him to the fire ring several feet away, watching as he relit the wood and wondering why he looked so serious. So this would not be another of their light, friendly conversations. She had a feeling she knew what topic he wanted to introduce, and instantly went on her guard.

nine

Nate warmed his hands over the small fire, enjoying its warmth and examining Carly in its flickering glow. She took a seat on a log across from him, her face a study of emotions. She may make a habit of tucking herself away in a private corner in an effort to hide from the world, but at times like now, she was easy to read. She acted as if she expected the worst, and Nate found himself in no better frame of mind. He took time to sort out what he wanted to say. When he had collected his words to the best of his ability, he shifted his position. Her gaze jumped from the fire to his face.

"I'd like to resume our conversation from where we left off."

"Yeah, I got the feeling this wasn't going to be a powwow to discuss the absence of the great fireball in the sky and the rain we've been having."

Despite the seriousness of the moment, Nate's lips curved into a faint smile at her choice of words. "What did you mean when you said you didn't get how we believed that God is always there to make things better?"

"You have a good memory." She prodded the dirt with the toe of her hiking shoe, looking at it. "I meant exactly what I said."

"Seems a little odd to have an attitude like that and be a member of Jill's church. On my visits there, I noticed they're a faith-believing bunch."

"I'm not a member of her church."

The words scraped like sharp pebbles in Nate's head. "Then why are you with the church group?"

"Why are you?"

"I was invited—by Ted."

"And Jill invited me." She shrugged. "She knew I needed a break from life and offered it."

"I see." He shut his eyes a moment to get his bearings. "So you don't believe in God." He posed the words as a statement; her attitude made it more than clear.

She eyed him with caution. "If I say I don't, you're not going to start preaching to me, are you?"

He gave her a sad smile. "No, Carly. I'm not going to preach to you. If you want to go get some shut-eye, I won't keep you any longer."

Rather than say good night and retreat to her tent, Carly surprised Nate by sitting motionless, a wistful look spreading across her face as she stared into the flames.

"The truth is before this hike, I could have said those words with conviction. But I don't feel that way anymore. I believe there is a God." Her midnight dark eyes lifted to his. "I'm just not so sure I want anything to do with Him."

At least she was honest and didn't try to fake something she didn't feel; he may not like her words, but he respected her forthright sincerity. His stepmother had woven a web of lies to trap his dad, who'd fallen for each one. Nate pressed his lips together in thought, wondering how to respond, when Carly spoke.

"I did once."

The three words jarred Nate. "What happened?"

She drew her knees up to her chest and locked her arms around her legs. "A little girl didn't get her prayers answered."

He waited, sensing more. He wasn't disappointed.

"When I was little, I used to curl up in my bed at night and pray that God would bring my mama back to me. My aunt never taught me to pray, but I'd seen kids do it in movies, and they always got what they wanted, so I prayed, too. I told Him I'd be good. I begged Him; I made deals with Him, anything to get out of my aunt's house and have my mama back." She grew very still, focused on the fire. "She did come back three times; I was twelve the last time. But each time she only stayed a few days, and she was always going on and on about some new boyfriend or a job she had at a nightclub or something else in her life that excluded me. She rarely noticed me except to ask if I'd been a good girl.

"That last time, I hadn't been, and my aunt let her know about it. My mama talked to me longer than she ever had and really paid attention to me because my aunt threatened to throw me back to her. But I didn't care that she was mad. I soaked up every moment of her sudden interest, and from that incident, I learned that bad girls get all the attention. So I began to live up to the name. If it was wrong, I did it. I didn't care."

She rested her chin on her knees. "Not that it did any good. Mama never came back, and after a while, I quit trying to be bad, quit hoping for something I realized wouldn't happen, and I quit praying to God. My aunt told me He didn't exist, and I figured she must be right."

Nate swallowed over the painful lump in his throat. At her wistful, childlike words and cheerless expression, he wanted nothing more than to enfold her in his arms. To pull her into a hug and kiss her, to let her know someone cared. And that was the problem: He cared too much.

Now that he recognized the truth concerning Carly's lack of faith, he knew that to go to her, to do those things, would invite disaster. He didn't want a relationship like his dad had. Nate had seen the results when what had appeared to his dad like nuggets of gold turned into fool's gold—something not worth all the pain he'd endured. To become involved with a woman who didn't share Nate's beliefs spelled danger.

He cleared his throat, uncertain of what to say. She lifted her head, spearing him with huge eyes that glimmered with unshed tears, and he felt as if his heart had been squeezed so he could barely breathe.

"She was wrong. I feel that now more than I know it. It's not logical after all. But at the same time, I'm not sure where I stand when it comes to making decisions."

He swallowed hard, recognizing the question in her statement. "It's a first step, Carly. Every important decision is arrived at one step at a time."

She chuckled. "Especially when traveling up a steep mountain."

He gave a wry grin. "Yeah, especially then."

She was silent a moment. "Honestly, Nate, I'm not sure what my destination will end up being in the grand scheme of things, but just so you know, I'm not a quitter when it comes to life. I may have given up believing my mother would return and given up on God, but on the things that really mattered— school, work, relationships—I always kept right on going no matter what."

Nate winced at her selection of words, but judging from her history, they came as no surprise. He weighed his reply.

"Carly, in your job as a reporter, you kept yourself well informed before writing your newspaper articles, right?"

"Well, I worked the entertainment section, so there weren't a lot of hot, juicy stories to be had, but yeah, I did."

Sidetracked for a moment, Nate homed in on her words. "If there was a hot, juicy story, would you have grabbed it?"

"What reporter wouldn't?" she laughed. "It's that type of story that gets a gal noticed and gains respect among her peers. Most people would rather read about what evils have hatched deep inside their town than read about who won the blue ribbon for the biggest zucchini or what band played at the Maple Syrup Harvest Festival. It's just human nature." She shrugged. "But Abernathy assigned me to entertainment, and what the boss says goes, so I never got my chance."

"Human nature can be cruel."

"It is cruel. That's just a fact of life. But it's a journalist's job to record all the facts and keep the public well informed."

"So if you still had your chance, would you take it?" The terse question left Nate's mouth before he could think to haul it back.

She seemed a little surprised. "I don't work at the paper anymore."

"There are others."

"But without credentials, I won't get far. Not unless I could present to the editor an exclusive headline story to hook interest. Don't think I haven't tried looking for work already. But Abernathy didn't send me off with any recommendations. Not after the scene I pulled at his office. Stupidity on my part, but what's done is done."

Nate took a steadying breath. He hadn't meant to get off on this track. With her curious nature, she probably felt more intrigued about his curt questions and behavior than ever before. He forced himself to switch back to the initial topic. This wasn't about him; this was about her.

"Like I said, Carly, you have to be well informed before you can make a good decision about anything in life."

She quirked her brows as he again switched the subject. "Okay, so?"

"So you might find the information needed if you attend the nightly Bible readings on a regular basis. I'm not trying to push you, just trying to help steer you where to look." He had noticed from the start that she didn't always show up at their group gatherings and should have realized something was amiss, but he had just assumed she was too exhausted or that she'd had some other logical excuse.

"I'll consider it."

That was all Nate had hoped for; at least she hadn't said no. He released a breath, smiled, and gave her a nod. "Well, it's getting late. I need to get some sleep." He stood up, noticing her expression of surprise, which she quickly masked. "I'll see you in the morning."

"Yeah, okay. See you."

Her words seemed faint, uncertain, but Nate didn't let himself turn around and ask why. The temptation to take her in his arms and hold her was still too strong.

&

The next morning, Jill insisted she could withstand the hike, though she didn't look much better. Kim seemed subdued, Frank appeared more tense than usual, and Ted acted almost scatterbrained. But the change in Nate baffled Carly more than anything else. He still acted as polite and helpful as ever, but he no longer sought her out. He rarely smiled, and when he did, it seemed almost sad.

She wondered whether his attitude had to do with her confession the night before, with Kim's disappearance, or with something else entirely. Their entire group seemed downcast after last night's frightening event, so maybe that was all that bothered him—the aftereffects and shock of what had happened and of what could have happened but didn't.

Carly still harbored surprise that she'd revealed so much about her past to Nate, since it had taken her months to leak the same information to Jill and Leslie. She'd known Nate a little over two weeks and had brought out every skeleton in her closet for his view, save for one. What was there about Nate that invited confidence? She had avoided this very thing, told herself she wanted to keep him at arms' length, and then, with little prodding on his part, she had revealed a good deal of her story.

Carly tried to ignore Nate and his sudden indifference to her, tried to pretend it didn't hurt. But it did. And she thought it an ironic twist that his distance irritated her more now than his constant shadowing had done during their first days of the hike.

They traveled a short, eight-mile distance that day, surprising Carly since Ted always pushed them. But the tough drill sergeant appeared to have softened around the edges, and Carly sensed he still worried about Jill.

"Tomorrow we tackle the Camel's Hump," he told the group. "It's above treeline, made of steep rock, and is as treacherous as all the stories you've heard. It's one long endurance test; I hope you're up for it."

As usual, Ted was all cheer and optimism as he prepared them for their next climb. Carly's gaze connected with Nate's, and he winked, sharing with her an amused smile. Carly felt lighter, though she hadn't yet shed her backpack.

After Carly deposited her things in the shelter, she looked at the mountain in the distance, which did resemble a camel's hump. Earlier, they'd run across the path of some hikers coming from Canada, who'd just tackled the treacherous mountain; one of the young men had slipped and fallen, banging up an elbow and badly scraping his leg.

"Nervous?" Kim came up beside her.

"About climbing the Hump?"

The girl nodded.

"Maybe a little. But if over three thousand people have tackled it, we can, too."

Kim flashed her a big smile, and that's when Carly noticed the elastic band that now secured the teen's glasses around her head.

"Smart add-on to the specs," she said.

"Yeah, Dad made it. He's good with putting things together from nothing."

Carly hesitated, remembering the night before. "Are things all right between you and your dad?"

"Sure. He was teed off at me; big surprise. But he's the greatest dad there is." Sincerity rang in Kim's voice. "He didn't want me to come on this hike, but I convinced him."

That surprised Carly almost as much as the wide variety of age groups she'd seen among those hiking the trail—from senior citizens to six-year-old twins backpacking with their parents. Kim appeared to be in good physical condition, an outdoor-type of girl. She had told Carly she'd played several sports at school.

"Why didn't your dad want you to come?"

Kim shrugged, seeming nervous. "Just didn't like the idea; I guess he didn't want the added hassle." She fidgeted with her walking stick. "I better go help Dad with dinner. See ya."

"Yeah, see ya," Carly answered pensively as she watched Kim head to the shelter where Frank had just emerged from the trees, hauling water.

"Heyo, what's up with you and Nate?" Jill asked, coming up behind her.

"How are you feeling?" Carly countered. "You still don't look in peak condition for the climb."

Jill answered her sad pun with a groan. "I'm bushed, but I'll live. This isn't the first time I've had to test my endurance beyond reason. The outback may not have as many places to climb, but it does have its challenges, and I managed twenty-three years Down Under. You've seen the movie *Crocodile Dundee*?"

Carly nodded.

"Well, I was more the Dundee type, and Ted the one I saved. From a black snake. . .deadset," Jill said, laughing at Carly's skeptical look and lifting her hand in a scout's-honor pledge. "Anyhoo, back to my question. What's with you and Nate?"

Carly had hoped she had successfully diverted the topic. "With us?"

"I sensed friction between you all day."

Carly snorted. "I have no idea. I made the mistake of telling him about my whole sordid life last night—well, not the part about Jake—and now he doesn't want anything to do with me." She shrugged. "It's for the best; I don't need any more hassles to complicate life."

"That's not like Nate." Jill looked puzzled. "I was hoping the two of you would be good friends."

Friends. Right. Carly gave a cynical smile. "Well, some things just aren't meant to be, Ju-Ju. I'm hungry. Let's eat while there's still enough daylight to see."

All through her preparation of vegetable stew via a food packet, Carly thought about Nate, wondering what she'd done to put the breach between them. He had seemed sympathetic last night, not judgmental—not that she wanted anyone's pity, either. She only wanted to understand what was going on between them and why she couldn't seem to get the guy out of her thoughts.

Growling to herself in frustration, she grabbed her mini recorder to document her day. Once she finished, she cleaned herself up as much as possible and laid her sleeping bag in the shelter. Tonight, she didn't want to be bothered with pitching her tent; a few in her group shared the idea, since she noticed their sleeping bags also laid on the wooden floor inside. Deciding to make it an early night, Carly settled in, thankful for her warm clothes and the insulation the sleeping bag gave.

A step at the entrance and a shadow alerted her to someone coming inside the shelter. From behind, the firelight glowed where the others held devotions, casting the face of the newcomer in darkness. Carly saw blond strands of hair and noted the curved outline.

"Kim? Is that you?"

"Yeah. Are you sleepy?"

Carly sat up. "Not if you want to talk."

Kim moved to Carly's sleeping bag and knelt down, sitting on her knees and tucking her hands between them. "I do, sorta. I feel closer to you than the other guys, and I need to talk to someone."

Carly tensed, thinking she knew what was coming. "Is it about your dad?" she prodded softly.

"My dad?" Kim sounded confused.

Carly bit her lip, not wanting to jump to conclusions. "Why not just tell me what's bothering you."

"I'm sort of scared about tomorrow."

"About climbing the Camel's Hump?" This, Carly had not expected. They had already managed some treacherous climbs, and Kim had never shown one ounce of fear but had always been the one ready to forge ahead.

"Yeah." Kim slumped down to a sitting position. "Remember when I told you the other night I was legally blind?"

"Yeah."

"Well, one day—soon I think—I'm going to be blind."

The shock of Kim's words robbed Carly of a reply.

"This hike was sort of a dream that I wanted to make come true before I lost my sight for good. And I'm glad I came. But the symptoms the doctor warned me about have started up, and now Dad's worried and wants to take me off the trail. But I don't want to go. I want to keep hiking to the border of Canada like my grandparents did. It's like one of those dream-wish sort of things to me."

She hesitated. "The other night when I got lost, the reason I tripped is because all of a sudden I couldn't see. It only lasted a couple of seconds, and according to the doctor, the disease gets progressively worse a little at a time and I won't go blind all at once. I should still have several weeks left. Even months."

"Isn't there an operation that can help you?" Carly forced the words out through a tight throat.

"Nothing that's even half of a guarantee. Or that isn't too risky. I've prayed about it a lot—Dad, too—and I just don't want to take those kinds of risks."

"But if there's a chance, isn't it worth the risk?"

"Hey, are you crying?" Kim sounded baffled. "Don't cry. I'm okay with it all, really. I just wanted someone else to know, maybe so you could be my cheering section. The others here don't know because we're still new to that church—we just moved to Goosebury a few months ago—and I didn't want anyone to know and then start getting all weird around me. People do that; all my friends in Massachusetts did. That's one reason we moved to Goosebury to be with my grandparents. I just want to be treated normal, and you always seem so together. I didn't think you'd get weird on me, too."

Carly didn't feel one bit together, and Kim was comforting her, which further addled her mind. In these past weeks of playing cards with Kim and getting to know her, she'd thought of the cheerful teen as the little sister she'd never had.

"How can you be so strong about all this? Why aren't you even the least bit angry?"

"At first I was. I threw a crying and shouting fit at home after the doctors told me, and I think if I didn't have Jesus to fall back on, I might still be really mad and never have left my room. I didn't for days. Sometimes I still get to feeling sorry for myself. But my relationship with the Lord has actually improved, and He's given me this strange sort of peace I never had before. Even before I found out."

"Kim, are you in there?" Frank's voice came from outside.

"Yeah, Dad, I'm coming," she called, then whispered to Carly, "He's still freaked out about last night, but anyway, now you know why." The teen hurried to her feet, leaving Carly shaken and far from feeling any peace.

ten

After devotions, Nate couldn't sleep and walked around the outskirts of the camp. He heard Frank call to Kim, saw the two leave the shelter area, and noticed they seemed to be having another heated conversation.

Ted clapped a hand on his shoulder, startling him. "Jill is feeling crook again. I don't want her to take the Hump, but she insists she can do it."

"Sorry to hear she's still sick."

"I'd like for us to pray for her tomorrow as a team. There's strength in numbers."

"Good idea. You want us to do that now?"

"No, everyone but you has turned in for the night." He paused. "So, what gives? Why are you prowling the area?"

Nate blew out a harsh breath, fisting his hands and shoving them into his pockets. "You didn't tell me Carly wasn't a member of your church group."

Ted seemed confused. "I didn't think it would matter."

His words sharpened Nate's disappointment to anger. "You didn't think it would matter to try to hook us up, knowing she wasn't a Christian, knowing what you know about my family and the hellish nightmare we're going through? That my dad's gone through for years?"

"Hey, man, chill out. I didn't know she wasn't a Christian. Jill met her when she was out shopping, but I don't hang with the women. I barely know Carly."

Nate forced himself to calm. "Sorry, Ted. I should've known better."

"But I'm really surprised Jill had a hand in this." Ted shook his head as if to clear it. "It's a good thing you found out before anything could happen. Now you know and can steer clear of entanglements."

"Yeah."

At the mockery in Nate's voice, Ted peered at his face. "Uh oh."

Nate let out a disgusted laugh resembling a snort. "You can say that again."

"You hardly know her."

Nate leveled a gaze at his friend. "How long did you tell me it took before you felt you loved Jill? Seven days?"

"Love. Oh, boy. Nate, I'm so sorry, man. If there's anything I can do. . ."

"Thanks. I have to work this one out for myself."

The two men parted, but rather than return to his tent, Nate used his flashlight as a guide to walk the perimeter of the campsite, needing to release his frustrated energy. After only an eight-mile hike that day, he didn't feel one bit exhausted, and his Carly-ridden thoughts strengthened when he remained motionless.

All day, he'd avoided Carly to the point of almost ignoring her, but he hadn't failed to notice her confused and hurt glances when she thought he didn't see. Turning a cold shoulder on her wasn't right, not after all the disappointments she'd suffered, and he didn't want to add to them and hurt her. Falling for her wasn't right, not after all the misery he'd endured, and he didn't want to add to that and hurt them both. Could he settle for in-between and just be a friend to her for the remainder of this hike, then part ways and forget about her?

He didn't need the Bible to tell him a Christian shouldn't get involved with a non-Christian; he'd had the proof in his own family and seen the dangers and results of conflicting faiths. Nate blew out a self-disgusted laugh. For the first time, he began to understand his dad instead of judging him. If his dad felt about Julia the way Nate was beginning to feel about Carly, then Nate could see how easy it was to reject what was right and embrace temptation.

Alerted to the sound of someone softly crying, Nate halted in shock. He followed the sound, his heart dropping when his flashlight picked up Carly. Her arm flew up over her eyes, and he dropped his flashlight's beam.

"Carly? What's wrong?" He thought about scolding her for taking off by herself, but curbed his words at the bleak despair in her eyes as they met his. She crossed her arms over her waist, clutching her elbows; she looked so vulnerable, so childlike, so desperate. So alone.

Her anguish tore at his heart until he felt her pain as if it were his. Without saying a word, he laid his hands against her back and drew her close. The dam broke as she let out gasping sobs, muffling them against his shirt. He lifted one hand to the back of her head, his hold tightening around her as he closed his eyes, wishing he could absorb her pain, wishing he could halt her tears while wondering what had caused them.

When at last Carly's tears dwindled to shuddering breaths, Nate smoothed his hand down her hair. "Okay, now?" he asked.

She sniffled and pulled away, wiping the back of her hand against her nose. "Yes, sorry. I should go back to the shelter."

"Do you want to talk about it?"

"I don't want to bother you."

Her words cut like knives, accusing him of his distant behavior. He felt their sharp sting to the core of his soul. No matter his personal feelings, he'd been wrong to ignore her, especially since he'd asked for her friendship.

"It's no bother."

At his quiet words, she looked up as if uncertain. Struck

anew, he felt as low as river algae. Had he put that hurt look in her expressive eyes?

"We're friends, Carly. It's okay." He made his decision.

A ghost of a smile lifted her lips. "Maybe I shouldn't tell you—she doesn't want everyone to know—but I can't handle this myself. It's all too much right now." He thought she might start crying again, but she straightened, then shook her head as if to stop it. "It's Kim. She's going blind."

"Blind?" Stunned, Nate watched Carly.

She nodded. "This hike is her dream wish. Nate, if there really is a God, how could He let this happen? Kim believes in Him. I feel as close to her as if she were my little sister; she's so special. When she told me tonight, I felt as if my heart might break. I still feel that way."

Her jumbled words made him swallow hard. He didn't know how to answer. But her grieving for Kim's sad situation made him realize what a sensitive and caring individual Carly was. Her first words questioning God's existence after telling him last night she'd come to believe it, then her next sentence proving she did believe it, showed him, too, that she was seeking. But seeking wasn't finding, and Nate cautioned himself.

"Carly, the answer to your question lies beyond my reach. Right now I'm going through some difficult times myself with my family and have tossed a few of my own questions up to God. I don't understand why some things happen, but I know that without Him, I'd be a lot worse off than I am now. So until I figure the reasons out—and I may never figure them out—I can only rely on Him as the safety harness to get me over the steep cliffs. I know that's the only way I'm going to make it. I don't know Kim well, but she seems tougher than she looks, and my guess is she's going to make it, too."

He didn't often speak of his faith and felt a little uneasy

under Carly's stare. She gave a slight nod, her eyes lowering to the ground. Silence stretched between them.

"It's late." Feeling he'd botched things, Nate decided to end this before he made it worse. "We have a hard climb tomorrow. I think we should both try to get some sleep."

Carly rubbed the moisture from her cheeks with both hands in one quick swipe. "You're right. I'm sorry."

"Don't be."

"Between my shedding tears all over you and ripping you with my talons, I've turned into quite a trail mate, haven't I?"

He gave a soft chuckle. "I've done my share of acting just as bad."

She looked anxious again. "You won't tell the others; I don't think Kim wants them to know yet."

"No, I won't tell anyone. It's her dad's place or hers to give out that kind of information."

"I wouldn't have said anything but—"

He sighed, realizing she'd taken his words wrong. "Sometimes heavy burdens need to be shared. Kim did that with you, and now you've done that with me. It's okay."

"Thanks, Nate." Her smile trembled, though her eyes shone and seemed more peaceful. "For being a friend."

They returned to the shelter, and she made her way past the sleeping campers to her bed roll, while he moved to his at the opposite wall. Once he settled inside it, he thought about their conversation and turned to glance at her in the dim lighting, but she'd turned her back to him. He looked away from her huddled form and to the peeled wooden logs above, reminding himself that friends were all they ever could be. He offered up a silent prayer for her, that she would find the answers needed; then he offered up another one for the brave teenager. Carly's words about Kim still stunned him, and he wondered why she'd told no one else of her condition. That she'd chosen to confide in Carly told Nate a lot, and he was glad others saw Carly's worth, too.

For the rest of their hike, he would continue being her trail mate and stow any mushrooming feelings far behind him, abandoning them on some lonely summit. He owed her that much.

❧

Fog and rain greeted them before they reached the Camel's Hump. Carly welcomed the bite of the stinging droplets on her skin; they helped to remind her she was alive. Kim, poor Kim, so young to go through something like this, too young. . .and Nate. She forced her mind to the treacherous climb of bare, treeless rock before her, but like the persistent droplets, the memory of his embrace lingered. . .his lips in her hair, his soothing voice, both hesitant and quietly commanding. A lifeline to help her pull herself together—she, who rarely fell apart.

These past two weeks had not only challenged her endurance, they'd stripped her of what she'd always considered her strengths, only to prove they were nothing more than weaknesses. Her callused view of life, her tenacity to forget the dull pain of the past while holding on to its brief sharp joys, laying brick by brick a wall of defense through her mockery of both herself and others. Hardened. Confident. Invincible. . . . Nate with slow persistence chipping away at the mortar that hid her miserable, dark soul—exposing her to light, sometimes without a word, sometimes with just a look. The wall flaking, herself trembling. Uncertain. Frightened. Vulnerable.

Her sole slipped on the slick rock, and she scrambled to get a hold, grabbing the jutting gray stone above to prevent her fall.

"Careful," she heard Nate's caution behind her.

Careful. She had tried to be cautious, to guard herself against him, but that hadn't prevented Nate from seeing through her farce or from her divulging secrets better left hidden behind her wall. Worse, a part of her cruel nature had welcomed the pain of baring her conscience to him, of the need to have him hear her confessions. In an act of self-punishment, she had hoped he might condemn her, might agree with her that her soul was as black as her aunt said, and yet the very thing that would disgust him, she had refrained from airing, unable to bear his judgment or the censure she was sure would chill his eyes. The distance he had put between them yesterday, the distance she had told herself she wanted, had made her heart ache with confusion and regret.

She didn't need this! Had done her best to avoid it. With Jake, she had been in love with the idea of being in love. In the sum total of the six months she had been with him, he had not once triggered the emotions that two weeks with Nate had produced. Had not once stirred, not only her flesh, but the core of her heart and soul, as well.

Carly gasped as the wall that surrounded her emotions crumbled further with the stark knowledge. She didn't want this! If she could, if there was a path, she'd leave the trail now and return to Goosebury. The withering judgment of the town would seem like balm compared to the torment going on inside her.

She told herself as they made the final ascent that she could handle one more week. At the summit, visibility was poor, but as close as Nate stood, their eyes connected, and she wondered if she believed her personal claim.

She loved him.

The wind had picked up speed, battering against them as they stood on the barren stretch of rock and took a break from climbing. But the thirty-mile-per-hour gusts that threatened to push them over the edge seemed inconsequential to the violent jumble of emotions that raged through her mind.

Her recognition of God's existence had somehow sneaked up on her, the awareness slow in coming; the realization that she loved Nate attacked her without warning as she climbed one of the most treacherous mountains on the trail. Both revelations scared her but for different reasons, and her mind felt as shaken as her body, now battered by the wind.

To escape the strong currents, Ted cut their rest short, and with the help of the white blazes on the rocks, they began their descent on the north side. The traction proved difficult, the rocks still wet though the rain had given over to mist. Carly concentrated every effort on where to place her feet and hands, not allowing her traitorous mind to heckle her further or to explore either well of revelation.

Halfway down the mountain, she lost her grip. She grabbed at the steep rock face, scraping her fingertips in a futile attempt to halt her slide of more than six feet on her stomach. Her sweatshirt rode up, the rocks biting into bare flesh. All at once, her soles thudded to a stop on a short ledge and stopped her fall into nothingness.

"Carly!"

She heard more scraping as Nate hurried his descent and landed beside her. "Are you okay?"

"Just a little shaken." More than a little. Her hands, chest, and legs stung with fire, and she trembled as much as her voice. She kept her gaze on the gray rock beneath her, her heart pounding with the fact that, except for one short ledge, she could have hurtled into oblivion.

Oblivion? Or was there more?

With a numb sort of shock, she watched Nate's hand pull her palm up. With him, she looked at the scrapes on her flesh. From the sticky feel, she was sure more of the same abrasions covered her skin below her jeans and sweatshirt.

"Do you need a minute to catch your breath?" His voice came very low, still.

She only wanted off this mountain and down onto level ground. She shook her head, trying to regain her confidence. With a shaky leg, she found a firm footing, beginning a much slower descent. Her body screamed from the pain of each action, and her mind reeled with the knowledge that this could have been more than just another fall. Only when she was again on safe ground did she let her mind continue its course.

Falls came with the territory; she had learned that these past seventeen days, since each of the group had endured their share. But this last fall had sent her close to hurtling off a mountain, and the shock of that made her throat tighten with apprehension.

She had always approached life with a devil-may-care attitude, certain once it ended, nothing else remained. Now she questioned that certainty, and with those questions came greater fears of the hell she'd heard mentioned. Fire and brimstone didn't sound like something she wanted to face, but she feared eternity held nothing more for her. She didn't need a Bible to tell her that her past sins were wrong; she'd known it deep inside. Otherwise, she would have felt no guilt, and she had. Each time.

Nate put a hand to her arm. "Are you okay?" The deep concern in his eyes moved her, shocked her. He looked as shaken as she felt.

"Falls happen." She tried to be glib with her answer, but he offered no answering smile.

"We can take it slower if you need to."

"I'm fine." She forced her lips into a facsimile of a smile. "Really." Without another word, she walked after the others. Yet her knees still shook, and throughout the rest of the hike to the next shelter, Carly revisited her near encounter with death.

That night after supper, Nate watched Carly and Kim approach their circle as the group prepared for devotions. Cheered that she'd made the choice to join them, Nate kept his expression calm as their eyes connected, and he gave a nod in greeting.

The barest smile touched her mouth before she sat beside Kim, only a few feet from Nate. The teenager was as bubbly and vivacious as ever, and Nate marveled at her strength, especially knowing what he now did about her disability. Both she and Jill had managed the Camel's Hump with few problems, Kim, with her youthful energy, raring to go once her feet touched level ground. Nate knew the prayers before the hike had aided in their success, and he was sure they'd saved Carly. Fresh panic rushed through his heart as he recalled the sound of cloth and buckles skidding on stone and the sight of Carly sliding toward the edge.

Each night, one of the group made a selection, and tonight as Sierra read a passage from the Gospel of John, Nate watched Carly. The hands, which had covered her knees so loosely before, tensed as her fingertips dug into her jeans. Her expression remained a blank mask, but in the flicker of campfire, he sensed moisture shimmering in her eyes. She whispered something to Kim, then rose and left.

Nate waited for her to return. He didn't think she would wander off, but as her assigned trail mate, he felt responsible. For all her brash independence and womanly strength, Carly had hidden away the hurting little girl from so many years ago, and he felt she'd just come to discover her on this hike. Personal epiphanies could do strange things to people, making them act contrary to their nature.

He gave her a few more minutes, then made his exit as Kim explained her views on Jesus's reactions in the passage. The shelter was dark, a few other campers already inside their sleeping bags. Nate headed in the direction he'd last seen Carly.

He wasn't sure what he expected to find, but when he spotted her sitting on the ground, dejected, her arms crossed on upraised knees, her head buried in them, he hesitated. He didn't think she was crying, but she looked beaten, like the loser of a long battle.

"Carly?" He whispered her name, afraid if he spoke too loudly, he might make her bolt like a frightened doe. A long, tense moment passed before she looked up.

eleven

Carly stared at Nate, resigned that he'd found her. He always did.

"I noticed you left and wondered what happened to you."

She offered a weak smile, the best she could do. Not even one of her usual flippant replies would surface to her brain.

"Is this about Kim?" he prodded, his voice still low as if afraid he might upset her.

She shook her head. "I'm still worried about her, sure, but no."

He moved closer and hunched down before her. "It might help to talk about it."

Why did he have to be so nice? It would have been so much easier if she'd ignored him all along like she'd planned to do, like she'd wanted to do, and if he'd kept his distance. It wasn't too late; she still held the key to drive him away. Once she told him, once she admitted her sins, then he would give her all the space she wanted. Her heart mocked her that now she was lying to herself, but her mind remained firm. She did want distance. She needed distance. Besides, once this hike ended, they would go their own ways. Her, back to Goosebury, and him, to wherever he came from. Suddenly she wanted to know.

"Where do you live?"

Her question took him by surprise; she could see that in the way his eyelids flicked up and how the soft rays of moonlight brought out the whites of them a little more. She was glad she sat in shadow so he couldn't see her as well as she could see him.

"Bridgedale."

"Is it far from here?"

"Southern Vermont."

She heard the puzzlement in his voice.

"Is Bridgedale a small town or a big city?"

"A small town."

"And are the people there as unforgiving as people in Goosebury? Are they as eager and ready to condemn a person for a stupid mistake when they probably do things just as bad?"

He grew so silent, she didn't think he would answer. "Bridgedale has its share of hypocrites. Unfortunately, there isn't a town called Hypocriteville for all of them to move to."

His voice came both tense and light, and she gave a half-amused chuckle at his remark. "But you're not one of them, are you, Nate? You don't judge a person by their faults, do you? No," she answered her own question. "You're not the type. At least I hope you're not the type."

Another tense round of silence. "Carly, where's this heading?"

"Good ol' honest Nate. Fair dinkum, Jill calls you. You're always so straightforward in your approach. Genuine, cutting straight to the chase. You would've made a good reporter, except you're just too nice. Reporters have to be tough sometimes, aggressive, mean. That's why I would've made a great one if I'd had a chance. I'm all those things. Good stories don't just fall into our laps, Nate, we have to pursue them, like a dog sinking its teeth into a mailman's trousers."

She wished the moon revealed his face better. When he didn't answer, she sighed, folding like a leaf under the weight of the rain. "You want to know where this is heading? All right, I'll tell you. That woman they talked about tonight, the adulteress Jesus saved from stoning? Well, that's me, Nate. Only it gets worse. I fell into that trap with the same guy—twice."

He didn't move, didn't breathe. She wished he would do something. Strike out with sharp, condemning words, clear his throat in nervousness, shake his head in a superior manner—anything!

"At the beginning, I saw the faded mark on his finger and asked about it. But he promised me he wasn't married, that it was from a class ring he no longer wore—he said the stone had come loose—and like a fool, I believed him, or that's what I told myself. Some things just didn't add up—his private calls on his cell when we were together, him living in the next town but never taking me to his home. I wrote our advice columnist at the paper to get some help, telling her he was married, though I didn't know for sure. Jake made me feel pretty and wanted—all lies, of course, to get what *he* wanted. I know that now. I found out a year and a half ago at the museum where I was doing an interview. I ran smack into him and his wife.

"You've heard of the expression 'the fur flew'?" Carly asked, then went on without waiting for an answer. "Once I made it obvious I was more than another art patron with my opening remark to Jake, she hit him with her purse, and he lost his balance and fell into a cordoned area." She laughed through her tears. "At that moment, I both admired the woman and despised her. I got my licks in, too, and threw the guidebook I was holding right at his gaping mouth."

She looked past the satisfying humor of seeing Jake sprawled at the foot of a painting of Mount Vesuvius and Pompeii, then grew serious. "We were both Jake's victims, his wife and I, and I swore I would never have anything to do with him again. But then he came to Goosebury several months ago, all penitent and charming. He told me his wife had left him, that he'd filed for divorce, and like a gullible fool, I believed him a second time. But I found out he had lied again—his wife phoned me at the office. That was the day I lost my job—I was so mad at him I ripped the phone from the wall and threw it on the floor. Later, Jake found me in the park, and we had it out. Our argument was overheard, and the rest, as they say, is history."

Nate's continued silence provoked Carly's irritation. "So

there you have it! Now you know the deep, dark sins of Carly; now you can brand me with your scarlet letter or throw rocks at me. There's plenty around, so why not just grab one and get it over with!"

He recoiled as if she'd hit him. "Throw rocks at you? Why would I want to do that?"

"Don't you get it, Nate? I'm that woman Sierra read about tonight. Even Jill doesn't know all my darkest secrets. No one does but you."

"Carly." His voice came very quiet. "Didn't you hear the rest of the passage? About how Jesus forgave and saved the woman, telling the mob that those without sin should be the ones to cast the first stone? No one did. That's because everyone sins and falls short of the mark."

"Even you, Nate?" she mocked. "You're so good. Surely you don't sin."

He sighed, and it sounded almost sad. "Everyone has sinned at one time or another. Being a Christian doesn't mean we do everything that's right and never slip up or miss the mark. It means we're forgiven and continue to allow Jesus to work through us. I still mess things up, Carly; I'm not perfect. But I know I have a Savior who's there, ready to forgive me when I turn back to Him and ask."

She froze, her mind refusing to believe what her heart had begun to hope. "God wouldn't want me, Nate."

"You're wrong, Carly. I think maybe He's the one who brought you here, away from everything else, so you could come to this point. I think He knew it was time, and you were ready to hear His message."

Tears glazed her eyes, and she flicked them away. Why was she always crying lately? This time on the trail she had probably cried more than she had in the last year.

"But if you want to know what I think—you weren't the

only one in the wrong. That lowlife boyfriend of yours is the real jerk as far as I'm concerned."

"He's not my boyfriend anymore. I never want to see him again. I may have been pretty loose and wild these past years, but the thought of being with another woman's husband makes even me sick. Especially since my mother did it. That's why my aunt hates me so much. On my thirteenth birthday, she couldn't wait to tell me what trash my mama and I both are and how my mama and uncle had an affair. Sometimes I wonder if I could be his daughter and that's why they took me in when Mama dumped me on them."

Nate became as still as if he'd been turned to stone. Shame washed through Carly at her outburst. If she could bite off her tongue, she would do it. Why had she said all that?

Nate cleared his throat, clearly ill at ease. Who could blame the poor guy? In this world with the slogan of "Do What You Like," her wild lifestyle wasn't a rarity except to the old gossips of Goosebury. And evidently to Nate. She had never been attacked with such fierce guilt before; Carly felt lower than she ever had in her entire miserable life.

"Carly, God hasn't seen or heard anything that will shock Him or keep Him from loving you. He doesn't ask you to clean yourself up before you come to Him; He asks that you come to Him and let Him clean you up."

Despite his calm words, her tears kept falling. She was glad she remained in shadow so he couldn't notice them.

"Nate." She worked to keep her voice steady. "For an entire lifetime, I was told there was no God. Lately, I've started changing my position on that. I appreciate what you're saying, but as the investigative type of person, I just can't accept what you say on blind faith. I need to dig in, to get the facts and see for myself."

"Then do it."

His three words took her aback, mirroring her earlier thoughts. "What?"

"You're a reporter; do what reporters do—dig in. The most realistic place to find out about God is in the Book of old records and documents, the Book that talks about Him. I have a pocket Testament if you want to borrow it. If you have questions, I'm here, and I know either Jill or Sierra would be happy to explain anything, too."

Stunned, Carly asked, "Why do you care so much?"

He glanced down before meeting her gaze. "We're friends, Carly. Friends care."

A painful lump lodged in her throat; she couldn't believe he would still consider her a friend after all she'd told him. "I'm not always a nice person, Nate. But you already know that by my attitude toward you those first days."

"Hey," his voice teased, "I thought we already put that behind us." When Carly remained silent, he went on. "Like I said, everyone occasionally misses the mark, Christian or not. No one here thinks any less of you, least of all me. Everyone has a bad day now and then."

Carly snorted. "That was more than one bad day, Nate."

"Week, then?" Nate flashed her a grin. "Believe me, I understand. I had a bad five minutes beside a creek once, and as far as I can tell, no one's held it against me. Come to think of it, I held her against me."

Shocked amusement chased away the gloom, and she swatted his arm. "I cannot believe you just said that."

"If you want the truth, neither can I. But then, I never said I was perfect."

She chuckled. "Okay, Nate. I accept the offer of your book."

He moved to his feet, holding out his arm. "Need a hand up? I think we should get back now. We don't want to start another panic like the other night."

Carly nodded and accepted his help, surprised she didn't want this talk with him to end. It had been one of the most emotional times of her life, one of the most shameful, one of the most awkward—and one she felt may have been the most important she had ever lived. Despite knowing her past, Nate still wanted her companionship.

He had not rejected her, had not thrown verbal rocks at her, had not eyed her with disgust. He had accepted her and offered his hand in friendship. He might not be perfect, but he came awfully close. And with another shock, Carly realized the only people who knew her secrets and still had shown her kindness were Christians: Leslie, Jill, and now Nate.

What made them different from the gossips in Goosebury, from her stern aunt, from her former coworkers who'd whispered behind her back? Was it their relationship with God? She had watched from a short distance that morning as the group stood in a circle, holding hands and praying for everyone, especially Jill. They'd then prayed for angels to guard their whole group as they hiked up the Hump. Carly thought about her near fall. Had an angel saved her from death, or had it been coincidence that the ledge had been there? Had God really cared enough about someone like her to assign a guardian to take care of her, despite all she'd said against Him in the past?

Once so sure she'd possessed all the logical answers, Carly now floundered at the unexpected questions.

ঌ

The next day, the climb loomed as hazardous as before, and the early morning rain didn't help. Whoever named the stretch of land a *trail* must not have known that *trail* implied something that could be hiked, whereas this northern section had to be climbed most of the time. Nate had expected it, though as a former section-hiker, he'd never traveled this far.

It was an obstacle course, the trail going up one side of a mountain, over nearly upright slabs of rock, then down the other side—dangerous for anyone, but especially an inexperienced climber. At one point, they had to descend a forty-five-foot ladder to get down a cliff. The going went much slower, everyone taking more care how and where they stepped. Nate forgot to breathe when Kim's foot slipped on the rung twenty feet above ground, but she managed to hold on and found a foothold, continuing the descent. Nate's heart pounded as Carly took the ladder. Every time she approached a dangerous descent, he held his breath, praying she would make it.

As she stepped onto safe ground—however "safe" ground could be on a mountain—he let out the breath he'd held. The last one down, he grabbed the ladder and began his descent. He never knew what happened. One minute, he had about six more rungs to go; the next, he lay sprawled on the ground, pain shooting through his backside.

"Nate!" All of a sudden, Carly knelt beside him, her hand on his shoulder. "Are you okay?" Concern flashed through her eyes.

"Yeah." He moved his legs to experiment. "Nothing feels broken." Except he felt like he'd fallen fifty feet and not five. "Just bruised."

Ted approached and offered him a hand. To Nate's surprise, Carly took his other arm, and they helped lift him to his feet. He winced and doubled over at the sudden pain shooting through his hip, but after a while, it faded to a degree that he felt he hadn't fractured it and could walk.

"Think you can continue?" Ted asked.

"What choice do I have?" Nate joked back. Secluded in the middle of the wilderness as they were, the only choice was to go forward.

As they continued their trek, he leaned on his walking stick until the fire eased into a sting. He noticed Carly's frequent glances over her shoulder, as if she were afraid he might suddenly fall off the mountain, and he recognized the irony that now she worried about him.

He hadn't been able to stop thinking about her when she was out of his sight, and when she was within sight, walking in front of him, it was worse. Every day, his feelings for her increased; every day, he wanted what he couldn't have.

Stupid, Nate. Really stupid. Hasn't your experience with your family taught you anything at all?

But. . .would it really be so bad? Carly was nothing like his stepmother. He'd never felt this strongly about anyone; even Susan had injured his pride more than she'd hurt his heart. But Carly. . .she was sincere, even if she did have some rough edges; compassionate, funny, smart, beautiful. . .would it really be so bad?

Nate already knew the answer, but his heart defied logic. Carly's story didn't shock him as much as she'd thought; he'd sown some wild oats before becoming a Christian, ones accepted by society as a whole but rejected by God. He hadn't been pure either, not until Jesus forgave him and washed away his sins with His saving mercy. And as Nate had told her, he still wasn't perfect. What shocked Nate had been the unspoken message she'd revealed through her rush of words— "I'm not worthy of love or forgiveness; I'm trash because my aunt says I am, because I had a relationship with a married man, because my uncle might really be my dad. . . ." The unspoken words had hit him harder than the spoken ones. In her mock indifference, as the tears glistened on her cheeks, he had glimpsed her genuine hurt and vulnerability. And at that moment, he'd known without a doubt: He loved Carly.

Since he'd come on the trail and reflected on the beauty

of nature all around him, since he'd taken part in the Bible readings and devotions each night, Nate had rediscovered the peace missing inside him for months, as well as a channel back to his Creator. He relied on that channel now.

"God," he said under his breath. "She's almost to the point of finding You; I can feel it. Maybe by dating her I could help be a better witness to her than I am now. Because if it really is so dangerous, if I could fall away from You by dating her and backslide, like losing my grip and falling down one of these mountains, then You're going to have zap these feelings I have for her out of me or send a chariot from the sky to sweep me off this trail."

Being with Carly every day—and her trail mate to boot—was slowly killing Nate's steadfast ability to resist temptation. Last night, as she'd sat there so sweet and lonely, all the while trying to act so strong and courageous, he could barely restrain himself from showing her just how much he cared by taking her in his arms and initiating another kiss. Their first kiss burned itself into his memory each night before he fell asleep and reminded his heart when he was awake and their eyes would by chance meet.

If only he'd known then what he knew now, he would never have let this happen; if only he'd known she wasn't with the church group and didn't share his faith, he would have been polite, yes, but certainly never kissed her. Yet he hadn't known. And that made him feel as if he'd been tricked—though he wasn't sure who to blame. Was it his fault he'd been ignorant of the facts and drawn close to her vibrant personality, seeking friendship? Was it his fault that he was a man, with all a man's feelings, and attracted to a very beautiful woman?

But you know now.

Nate shut out the small whisper and concentrated on the next climb.

twelve

Carly didn't know what was wrong with her; she felt restless even after having just hiked up a mountain with gusts of wind at gale force almost knocking them down. They'd had to stop at points so as not to be blown off the mountain. Her respect for hikers intensified each day she spent challenging "the beast" as Bart had dubbed the precarious path of steep mountains. At Profanity Trail, it hadn't taken three guesses to know why it had been given such a name. She looked, stomach plummeting, at what had been termed so carelessly the Chin. Devil's Drop might have been a more accurate name for it.

The trail descended straight down the side of a mountain, with treacherous sections that stood perpendicular, each of them at least fifteen feet wide. One slip of the foot and her near miss of the other day would become a reality.

"And I came on this hike, why?" she wryly muttered to herself.

"You okay?"

She looked at Nate. His face bore a look of concern as if he could read her mind. "Well, I always wanted an adventure; I got one."

He cracked a grin. "A little adventure can be fun. You'll do fine. And remember, I'm right behind you."

For some reason, his words gave Carly the added boost she needed, though if she fell into him, they would both go hurtling off the mountain. Still, to know he was behind her, supporting her, helped.

It took their group over an hour to ford the Chin, no more

than half a mile in length. Everyone made it without mishap, and a lot of backslapping and smiles floated around. Jill offered a short prayer of thanks. Carly had grown accustomed to hearing them pray for each other, for the group, for the hike, even for other campers each morning and evening. What once made her uneasy and desire an escape now made her watch with frank interest. She'd read some of Nate's New Testament the night before and couldn't wait to get Nate alone. She realized she could ask her questions of the group and they wouldn't mind, but she didn't feel comfortable with that idea yet. First she wanted to see how Nate responded to her queries. Jill still looked too shaky and pale, and Carly worried that her friend continued to fight the lasting effects of whatever virus had attacked her. At the shelters, Jill often excused herself early and crawled into her tent to rest, so Carly didn't want to bother her.

Once they arrived at Sterling Pond Shelter, Carly felt they'd reached the proverbial calm oasis after the steep barren stretches of windy mountain. The tranquil area was a treat for the eyes and a balm to the soul. The pond, a shimmering glacial lake, sat atop the mountain and seemed almost surreal, a pleasant dream after the day's nightmare of a climb.

Carly shrugged off her backpack and ate, feasting on healthy snacks rather than exerting more energy to cook a meal. Day after tomorrow, they would reach another predesignated food drop, and Carly had ended up packing too much food, as she'd been told many hikers did.

She sat by the pond, enjoying the cold breeze that ruffled her hair and the white cirrus clouds in the blue sky before dusk. Nate joined her. She lifted a slim packet from her backpack.

"Want a protein shake?" she asked innocently. "I'm trying to cut down on what's in my backpack."

His brows lifted. "Are you sure you aren't trying to kill me, then hide the body to create your own headline story?"

Laughing, she choked on a sip of her shake. "Oh, come on, Nate. It's not that bad."

"You're right. It's worse." He grinned. "So, after experiencing the Chin, you ready for tomorrow? Whiteface Mountain is a tough climb."

"Worse than what we've already been through?" Carly doubted it could get much worse.

Nate shrugged. "So I've been told. Ted and I only section-hiked it years ago. I've never hiked the whole trail at once."

Knowing he was also a first-timer at thru-hiking made Carly smile. "I read part of your book last night."

"Oh?" Evident interest lit his eyes, but he didn't push, instead waiting for her to offer information. Carly liked that about him, though she was just the opposite.

"There's something I don't understand. Well, more than one thing, really. If the Father—God—is so good, why would He want to kill His only Son? Why did He allow that to happen? That doesn't seem like a good thing to me. Weren't there other ways to work things out?"

Nate hesitated, as if gathering an answer in his mind. "Jesus freely gave up His life, since His Father willed it of Him, and He loves the Father, just as the Father loves Him. Men loved sin, and that separated us from God. Blood is sacred to God, and a perfect sacrifice was the only way to save us so we could be with Him."

He hesitated. "I don't want to sound like I'm preaching."

"No, please, go on. I asked." Carly wasn't sure why, but she didn't mind Nate explaining things to her.

He smiled. "Okay, then. God loves us, but sin kept us away from Him and from every good thing He has for us. Sin is like a chasm between mountains, with no way to the other side. It's like we're stuck on one steep and windy mountain with its sheer drop-off to death, but we're unable to reach the next mountain to find cool, refreshing water."

Carly nodded, glancing toward the peaceful pond, then back to Nate.

"Despite the wickedness of men, God looked beyond that and wanted His creation—us—with Him. He loved us that much. But He is so good, so holy. And just as where light is, there can't be darkness, where He is, there can't be sin. So He formed a plan from the foundation of the world, knowing what would happen to us, how sin would claim us. . . . Have I lost you yet?"

She shook her head, entranced. "Not at all. Go on."

"Jesus became the blood sacrifice, sacred to God. In the Old Testament, they sacrificed unblemished goats and sheep—that was a foreshadowing of Jesus yet to come. He was the ultimate sacrifice; only His death didn't just atone for people's sins, like the sheep's did; His blood washed the sins away like a pure, strong rain causes the dirt to wash from the rocks and makes them gleam when the sun comes out. Because He was pure and without sin, His blood was pure. There's a verse in Isaiah I learned that helped me when I was a new Christian: 'Though your sins be as scarlet, they shall be as white as snow.'"

His quiet words fascinated her, bringing a catch to her throat and the sting of tears to the backs of her eyes. "Thanks, Nate. I think I understand a little better now."

They talked more about it until dusk darkened the clouds. The group began to gather in a circle for devotions. Nate stood to join them and held out his hand to Carly, an open, silent invitation. She glanced at the calm, refreshing water, then back at Nate and gave a little nod. Taking his hand, she allowed him to help her to her feet.

❧

Nate listened in amazement as Carly drilled the group with

question after question about the reading Bart chose. She wanted to know why the Jewish rulers condemned Jesus when there was so much proof He was a "good guy" because of the healings He'd done and the people He'd brought back to life. She wanted to know why His own hometown didn't accept Him since they'd seen all His works and wondered how they could explain such evidence away. She wondered how His own brothers and sisters couldn't tell who He was when their mother so obviously knew and probably had told them. Once someone would answer, she'd pop back with another question, not to start a debate, but in a candid desire to get all the facts.

Some of her questions were brilliant, others might have seemed ignorant or silly to some who'd been in the Christian faith for a while, but to Nate they were all significant evidence that she was searching and trying to understand. He didn't treat her or her questions with anything but the utmost respect, as the entire group did. Devotions forgotten, she continued popping the questions out until long after dark.

Ted brought a halt to the evening, reminding them they had another difficult climb tomorrow, and many groaned.

"I warned you sluggards what you were up against at the beginning of the trip," he said, and Nate felt sure he wasn't the only one who would like to give their cheerful drill sergeant a good dunk in the glacial pond.

Ted looked at Carly. "If you're ever interested in joining our Bible studies once we get back home, we meet at our house on Wednesday nights. I'll bet you could bring a whole new perspective to things and get all of us in the Word digging for answers. You sure know how to make a person think."

She shrugged. "I guess it comes with the territory of being an ex-reporter. We're pretty hard-nosed. We don't give up until we find the answers we're looking for."

Her words twisted inside Nate, giving him yet another good

reason to write off Carly Alden as a potential girlfriend. If he were smart, once this hike ended, he would create distance instead of tossing around the idea of asking for her e-mail address. She'd always wanted a headline story to secure a coveted position as a journalist at a newspaper office—at least that's what she'd told him. And a one-on-one, exclusive interview with the stepbrother of the juvenile felon who'd burglarized a convenience store and killed the town's most beloved cop, along with wounding two other policemen and several civilians during his car chase getaway, would be too juicy a morsel for her to pass up, Nate was sure.

Forget about her, Nate. Pray for her, hope the best for her, but forget about her.

Again, his heart wouldn't listen.

thirteen

Carly wasn't sure if the climb up Whiteface Mountain seemed so rough because they were all weary from climbing for days or if it really was one of the worst mountains they'd encountered. At least the sun had dried the rain from the rocks, and a number of handholds jutted out for them to grab onto. No mishaps occurred, and the group breathed a collective sigh once they made their descent on the other side.

"Only sixty-two miles to go," Nate said.

Carly twisted to look back at him. "Go where?"

"The Canadian border. We're nearing the end of the trail, Carly."

"I can hardly believe it." Had they really come so far? Mixed feelings of relief, jubilation, and regret swept through her, leaving her almost dizzy. Or maybe that stemmed from the aftereffects of the climb.

And what of Nate; would he shake her hand and return to Bridgedale once they reached trail's end? Of course he would; it was where he belonged, just as she belonged in Goosebury. They would wish each other well and go their separate ways. Once apart from him, she would get over this ridiculous, mad, "swoonable" desire for Nate to take her in his arms and kiss her as he had that day in the rain and then tell her he wanted more than friendship.

The altitude must have finally gotten to her head for her to entertain such crazy thoughts. What the rocks and mountains had done in battering her body, her mind had done to her heart, thinking up all manner of ridiculous scenarios. Once she found level ground again, things would settle back on an even keel. At least she could hope.

ⱥ

At Bear Hollow Shelter, Nate pitched his tent and found the spring so he could retrieve some water. Jill was already there for the same reason. She straightened when she heard him approach.

"Heyo." She smiled, though he noted the strain around her mouth. It had been a hard trail for her, for all of them. "You all right, mate?"

He withheld a wry chuckle at the idea of being "all right" and filled his containers. "How long have you known Carly?"

"Half a year. Why?"

"This Jake character." Nate could barely get the name out without clenching his teeth. "Is he a threat to her?"

"Other than hounding her to death, no. He's a mongrel, that one, the most despicable person alive." Jill studied him, her gaze intent.

Nate came alert. "He's come after her? Stalking her?"

"I wouldn't say stalking, but he won't leave her alone." Jill bit her lower lip, then let it loose. "Nate. . ."

"That's not good." His jaw tensed. "She's looking for answers. I hope she joins your Bible studies once you return to Goosebury."

"What's going on between you two?" Her voice was very quiet.

Mockery made him raise his brow. "Going on between us?"

"Carly never would have told anyone about Jake. . .unless. . ."

"Unless she had good reason to?" he finished for her.

She inhaled a swift breath. "I never meant. . ." She didn't finish.

"Never meant what, Jill? To push us at each other? To make us trail mates so we would have to spend time alone together?

Or you never meant that I should fall in love with her?"

"Oh, Nate."

He shook his head. "You knew better. And still you did it."

"I just wanted you to be good mates. Carly needs them; she's so lonely, though she won't admit it, and I felt you two would get along. As good mates, only that."

He gave her a steady look, and she lowered her gaze as if ashamed. "I guess I overshot my mark."

"Maybe just a bit." His voice was grim.

"I never dreamed Carly would want more than friendship, what with the way she feels about blokes right now and all she's been through, and I knew you'd just broken up with a sheila, so I didn't think you'd be interested. . . ." She bit her lip again. "How does she feel about you?"

He sighed, looking at the water. "I haven't asked and don't feel I should. But one thing's clear: She no longer rejects my company."

"I'm so sorry, Nate. I should've told you about Carly from the start. It's just I never thought. . ." Tears trembled in her voice. "What will you do?"

"Do?" Bitter irony twisted his words. "Well, as I see it I have two options. I can toss everything I know is right to the wind and do what my dad did and pursue this, hoping against hope it doesn't turn out bad like it did for him. Or I can cut my heart out of my chest and walk around half empty, hoping God'll somehow fill the void."

She gasped. "You've known her less than three weeks."

His gaze shifted to hers, somber. "And you knew Ted less than that. Deadset?"

"Deadset," she whispered.

Seeing tears glisten and one drop down her cheek, Nate felt like a worm, but he was too upset to withhold his words. He just managed to keep his tone quiet. "I've never felt about anyone the way I do about Carly. And now, no matter what decision I make, I'll suffer for it, and Carly will, too."

"Nate, I don't know what to say. I'm sorry. I'm sure if you ask, God will help you over this hump, too."

He only looked at her, and she lowered her head. "I'll pray for you."

"Thanks." Again, he couldn't keep the mockery out of his voice, and when she turned and hurried away, he felt like a heel.

It wasn't all Jill's fault. He had seen a few warning signs—Carly's absence from Bible studies the first few nights, her lack of participation when she did join the group. He just hadn't looked hard enough to recognize those signs for what they were.

"Nate?"

Hearing her voice, he tensed. She walked toward him, her expression concerned.

"Is Jill okay? I just saw her coming from this direction, and she seemed to be crying. Before I could ask her, she went inside her tent."

Worm and heel were words too nice for Nate. *Algae* worked better.

"I may have said something to upset her."

"You, Nate?" Her full lips tilted into a soft, incredulous smile and drew Nate's eyes to them. "Somehow I doubt that. You're too nice a guy."

His mind already wrapped up in Carly, who now stood so close, Nate didn't return her smile as he again looked into her dark eyes. "You wouldn't say that if you knew what I was thinking right now."

Her smile faded as her lips parted, her expression one of dawning shock and revelation. Her night-dark eyes glistened with a mix of anticipation and fear. She lifted her face, just a fraction, and he realized with a jolt that she *wanted* him to kiss her.

The awareness made withdrawing that much more difficult. Nate struggled within himself, his jaw flexing hard, the pull toward Carly strong. . .too strong. His fingers lifted to brush her satin cheek, stopping at her jaw, and he slowly leaned in toward her.

"Carly!"

Jill's voice broke them from the spell. Carly jumped and turned as Nate dropped his hand to his side.

"I need your help, luv. It'll just take a few minutes."

"Sure." Carly appeared confused and again looked at Nate. She opened her mouth as if to say something, then just shrugged with a little smile and hurried away.

Nate closed his eyes, realizing how close he'd come to the brink. His mind knew profound gratitude, his heart only anger that Jill had pulled him back just in time. He couldn't go on like this, torn between right and wrong from moment to moment, tempted on a twenty-four-hour basis. The newfound peace he'd discovered with God these past weeks seemed to shatter into fragments inside him.

In the Bible passage they'd read when they first started this hike, the apostle Paul wrote that he waged war against the law of his mind, making himself a prisoner of sin and allowing sin to work in his members, saying what a wretched man he was since he desired to do what was right, but his body kept doing what was wrong. Nate now understood the man's plight. He seemed to have no control over his body, over his heart, regardless of his spirit's warnings of what he knew to be acceptable. And no matter how hard he tried to pretty the picture of having a relationship with an unbeliever, the canvas remained bleak and gray.

"I can't keep this up, God, not for another week. And I

don't see any chariots coming from the sky to cart me away, either. Give me what I need to do Your will, since You haven't killed these feelings inside me like I asked. If anything, they're stronger than ever."

He couldn't help his bitter prayer. Right now, he hurt, and he'd always been open with God, never hiding or pretending. His Creator knew him inside out. He knew just how much Nate wanted Carly, knew just how much he desired to take her in his arms and show her. . . .

And Nate knew the next time an opportunity came, Jill might not be around to stop it.

❧

Sierra approached Carly as they readied for their hike the next morning.

"I just want to tell you how much I enjoyed meeting you and getting to know you, Carly. When we reach Johnson today, Bart and I are leaving the trail. That tumble he took yesterday hurt his ankle, and he can barely walk on it, it's so swollen."

"You're not finishing the hike?"

"We just can't. I don't think he can make the next fifty-four miles, and he's happy to call it quits. I'm thrilled we made it this far; it's been an experience I'll never forget. We came to find a better connection with nature, with God, and with each other. And I think we did all that and more. We may be newlyweds, but we've known each other forever, it seems." She laughed. "We were high school sweethearts. And even though we only got married a few months ago, we were already comfortable around each other, maybe too comfortable. We took each other for granted, and this hike has helped us to better appreciate each other."

"That's great, Cat. I'm happy for you." Carly was but couldn't help feel a twinge of jealousy. She would love to have the kind of relationship Sierra and Bart had, if she ever did decide to start a relationship with someone again. Unwanted, an image of Nate came to mind, and she shut her mental blinds over it. "I wish you the best. Be sure and come to the Native American art exhibit I told you about next month."

"Bart and I talked about it, and we definitely want to go. And Carly, you really should consider coming to one of the Bible studies at Jill's. We have such fun there. We read, we discuss, we pray. But we have dinner before that and end the night shooting pool in Ted's game room. We have a sort of running challenge—the guys against the girls in eight ball. Losers wash the dishes. Of course, we girls always win."

Sierra winked, and Carly laughed. The idea didn't sound as distasteful to her as it might have weeks ago. These people had become her friends, and she welcomed the opportunity to see them again.

"E-mail me any time. Jill has the address. Maybe we can do lunch sometime, too." The women hugged, then along with everyone prepared to leave the campsite. When the group gathered to pray for a safe day's hike, Carly decided to join them. No one looked shocked, and Carly felt grateful for that.

Nate seemed tense, but he smiled when she greeted him. She yearned to ask about his bizarre behavior the night before, her heart leaping at the memory of the kiss he'd almost given her, but instead she made a silly remark that soon she would resupply her protein shakes and had plenty to spare any time Nate wanted one, to which Nate gave a taut chuckle. She didn't understand the sudden friction she sensed between them, though he still conversed with her in an easy manner.

Their hike seemed to go faster, cheerier, or maybe the group's general mood had changed, knowing they would soon reach civilization if only for a short time. They trekked four miles to the trail turnoff at the main road and made it into Johnson early in the afternoon.

At the sight of a supermarket, Laundromats, a drugstore, and other welcome beacons of civilization, each of the group went their own way to tackle priority lists. For Carly, that included food—real food—and picking up new batteries for her mini recorder. While inside the drugstore, she noticed Nate head for one of the outside payphones, probably to call home.

A thread of guilt wound around her conscience that she hadn't done the same, and she grabbed a couple of postcards to put with her purchases, intending to jot notes off to Leslie and Blaine, and even her aunt, while she took advantage of the local Laundromat. Not that Carly felt Aunt Dorothy would care if she fell off a mountain or made it back to Goosebury in one piece, but she should at least send a postcard for the sake of her young cousin, who didn't treat her like ragweed and often enjoyed sneaking up to Carly's attic room at night and talking with her. Maybe that's why she felt so attached to Kim; though Trina had a more somber, detached personality, almost gothic, the teenagers were close to the same age and had both latched onto Carly.

After paying for her purchases, she took her bag and juice and left the building. Her attention shifted to Nate, who stood tensed against a phone stand, clutching its metal side with a white-knuckled hand. His other hand gripped the receiver to his ear; his eyes when they met hers seemed apprehensive.

"Nate?" she whispered. Without thought, she shifted the bag to her other hand and touched his arm in concern.

He shook his head, showing he couldn't yet talk, and continued to listen to whoever was on the other line.

"Just how bad is he?" He waited, his jaw clenching. "Well, what can you tell me, Julia?" He rolled his eyes closed then open in barely concealed patience. "Yes. . .yes, I understand. No, I won't. I'll be there as soon as I can catch a bus back." He blew out a rapid breath. "No, Julia, I'm sure you weren't to blame for any of it. I need to get off the phone now so I can make arrangements. Good-bye."

Nate hung up and looked at Carly. Her heart beat fast at the pain in his eyes. "It's my dad," he said, his jaw flexing. "He had a heart attack three days ago."

"Oh, Nate. . ." Her hold on his arm tightened. "I'm sorry. Is it bad?" She winced at her stupid question; of course it was bad for Nate to be looking this white.

"He's in critical condition. Complications developed. I need to get back to Bridgedale."

She nodded. "Anything I can do to help?"

His expression softened as if shocked and amazed by her offer. "Yeah. If you would let Ted know, I'd appreciate it. I heard him say he was heading for the supermarket. I need to make arrangements to find a way out of here."

"Sierra and Bart are leaving the trail today, too. They might be able to help."

"I'll meet up with them." Still, he stood there, his expression blank.

She set down her bag and offered him her drink. "You look like you could use a perk."

He took the drink she offered with a measure of wary curiosity.

"It's just orange juice. No seaweed in it. Promise."

"Seaweed?"

"Kelp."

"Ah." His manner distant, he nodded one brief time as if figuring something out. "Seaweed." He spoke as though not aware of what he said, as if his mind operated in some other realm.

He took a few thirsty swallows, then handed it back to her. "I need to go make plans for finding a way back home."

"Plans can wait a few minutes," Carly said, injecting calm

authority into her words. "You still look shaky. What kind of trail mate would I be if I let you go off like this?" she joked. Not spotting any type of bench, she took his arm to move with him to the curb. "Just sit down awhile, until you feel more grounded." She didn't give him the chance to refuse. She sat by the side of the street, pulling him down beside her. Lowering his head, he propped his forearms on his widespread knees in dejection.

"I should have been there for him, Carly," he said after a moment, his voice husky. "He came to see me at my apartment the day I left for the hike; he needed me then, but I couldn't take hearing more of the same. I walked out, actually left him sitting there on my bed, and told him to lock the door before he left." He shook his head. "I didn't want to hear anything he had to say."

She hesitated, considering the action, then slid her arm around his shoulders. "Nate, you couldn't have known this would happen. If you had stayed home, it probably still would have happened."

When he didn't respond, she continued. "You told me a few days ago this hike has done a lot for you and has blown away the cobwebs from your mind—reenergized your spirit. I think that's how you put it. If you hadn't taken this hike, you might still be in the position you were then. Now you've got more clarity of mind and maybe could be a better help to your dad and your family than you would have been had you stayed."

He sat still a moment before turning his head to look at her. "Thanks."

A wealth of emotion infused his simple word, and Carly nodded.

They sat in silence for a few minutes, sharing her orange juice. When he again stood, Carly was grateful to see more color in his face.

"I need to get started."

"I'll go find Ted."

Nate nodded, and Carly wondered if this was the last she would ever see of him. Somehow, it didn't seem the right time to ask.

Thirty minutes later as the group convened for good-byes, she received her answer. Bart, Sierra, and Nate shook hands and accepted hugs all around. When Nate stopped in front of Carly, she looked up, wondering which form of farewell he would choose. He did neither, only stared into her eyes. The others moved away as if to give them time alone.

"I'll never forget this hike, Carly, or you."

His words rang clear with a final farewell and answered another of her unspoken questions. She had expected this, always knew the end of their trail together would come; she just never realized the reality would hurt so much.

Swallowing over the lump in her throat, she foraged around in her backpack and pulled out his pocket Testament, handing it to him.

"Thanks for the loan."

His eyes lowered to the black book, stayed there a few seconds, then lifted to hers again. "Keep it. And, Carly?"

She tilted her head, waiting, her heart speeding up at the intense but gentle expression in his blue-gray eyes. Nate hesitated as if trying to make a decision about something. Then, with a touch barely there, he clasped her arms and leaned down to press his warm lips to her forehead.

"Never give up your search."

Unable to find her voice, she gave a slight nod. With a tight smile and answering nod, he turned away to join Bart and Sierra. As Nate hoisted his backpack up and walked off with the couple, Carly stared after him, a film of tears clouding her vision.

"Good-bye, Nate. I'll never forget you, either," she whispered.

fourteen

The hike didn't become any easier, but it did grow less crowded on the northern section of the Long Trail. In the evenings, Carly took out Nate's New Testament, running her fingers along the worn edges and over his name that he'd penned on the first page. Holding his book helped her feel close to him. Two days had passed since he'd left, and she felt as if her heart had a hollowed void. She missed their lively banter, his teasing grin, the breathless way her heart caught when their eyes met. Even those first few frustrating days with him had mellowed into a pleasant memory, often bringing a chuckle or making her pulse race when she remembered those moments by both streams. . .and their kiss. A kiss that had caused her heart to pound, making her feel warm and alive, yet protected and cherished.

By the beam of her flashlight, Carly read the tiny print. Being a fast reader, she started at the beginning once more and whipped through all four Gospels in two nights. Some of the things Jesus told His disciples and others sent a shiver of awareness down her spine. His ancient words mirrored the way events happened in the twenty-first century, bringing the book to life in a way Carly never would have dreamed that documents written over two thousand years ago could do.

Fascinated to see the parallels, she soaked up the words of and about Jesus, not understanding the entire message but able to grasp a good deal of it. Each time she reached the Crucifixion, the manner in which the people treated Jesus appalled her. The account of His Resurrection sounded too farfetched to believe, yet the words tugged at her, not allowing her to discredit them so easily.

She joined in the group discussions and asked pointed and deep questions as if she were interviewing Ted and Jill, Kim and Frank. They answered to the best of their ability, often pacifying Carly, sometimes confusing her.

The third night on the trail since they'd left Johnson, Jill approached Carly as she closed the pocket Testament and stared into the fire. Jill winced as she sat down.

"You okay?" Carly worried because Jill had never regained her rosy complexion.

"Between you and me? No. I'm bushed. Only God's grace is getting me through this hike. I'm still crook. Ted wants me to see a doctor once we get back."

"Good for him. At least we're almost at the end of the trail."

"Too right." She looked at the Testament in Carly's hands. Carly followed her gaze, then smiled at Jill.

"Nate gave it to me."

Jill nodded, a somber expression in her eyes. "You miss him, don't you?"

"Am I that transparent? I need to work on that. I used to be as solid as a brick wall."

"Not all walls are good to have, Carly."

Carly snorted and looked into the fire, shaking her head. "Ju-Ju, if I told you my deepest, darkest secrets, you'd be sorry you even knew me."

"I doubt that. Give me a fair go."

And suddenly tired of hiding, Carly did. She told Jill everything she'd told Nate. . .and more. She confessed her disgusting attitude and her despicable acts, going as far back as high school. She admitted her hatred of her aunt and uncle, and why, and also her bitterness and hatred toward her mom. Strangely, baring those restricted feelings from her past to her friend brought satisfaction. The words were dark, but she felt lighter.

Jill stared at her, her expression unchanged. "And you think that makes you unlovable how?"

Carly blinked. "Didn't you hear a word I just said?"

"I heard, but it's you who needs to listen."

"What?"

"Carly, before I became a Christian, I was a bartender in my poppy's boozer—not enough to make a quid, but I didn't care. I was, shall we say, more than mates with some of the blokes there. I drank, I smoked, I raged on till all hours of the night and often past them. . . ."

As Jill continued recounting her life, Carly stared, unable to link the wild girl described with the quiet one who sat before her now.

"So you see, no one lacks a past, even Christians," Jill concluded. "Some pasts are nastier than others, but it takes one step to forgiveness—asking for it and accepting Jesus as your Savior. The day that happens, God wipes the slate of your life clean, and you start fresh with no past as far as He's concerned. No worries."

"So, after all that's done, you stop making mistakes?"

Jill blushed. "No. I made a doozer of one just this month, but I know I have a loving Father who forgives and waits for me to ask Him to step in, and I have. I've prayed that He somehow fixes my blunder to His satisfaction."

"What blunder?"

Jill shook her head. "Maybe I'll tell you someday; not yet."

❧

Nate sat beside the hospital bed and watched his dad open his eyes. Relief surged through him.

"You know, Dad, if you really didn't want me to go on the hike you could have just told me."

At Nate's light words cloaking two days and nights worth of worry, his dad let out a faint laugh, then grimaced.

"Sorry. After you've just had triple-bypass surgery, I shouldn't crack jokes. How are you feeling?"

"Like someone took a can opener to my chest."

"Not far from the truth." Noticing his father's eyes dart past him and around the room, Nate added, "Julia left to get something to eat."

"I'm surprised she stayed. A couple of days before I collapsed, she threatened to leave me."

That didn't shock Nate, and he felt briefly remorseful that he wished the woman had walked out of his dad's life. He talked a bit more before his father grew less lucid and closed his eyes again.

Throughout the next few hours, Nate tried to read a sports magazine, tried to watch news on TV, and consulted with doctors and nurses who slipped inside to tend to their duties. His mind seesawed between thoughts of the man in the hospital bed before him and thoughts of the woman he'd left behind on the trail. He prayed for Carly often, asking the Lord to open her eyes to the words in his pocket Testament. He hoped that, with time, his feelings for her would fade. If she did become a Christian, he would renew their acquaintance in a heartbeat, but that was a dangerous road for his mind to travel. He couldn't plan his future on a possibility.

Next time his father awoke, they engaged in brief conversation before Julia swept into the room. Nate tried to give her the benefit of the doubt, tried not to judge too harshly, but he couldn't help comparing her superficial, self-centered conversation to Carly's worries about Kim and others. Two nurses came in, asking them to leave for a few minutes, and Julia and Nate walked into the corridor. She surprised him when she clutched his arm, worry lines apparent on her face.

For the first time, he wondered if her calm demeanor in the room had been an act so as not to upset his father.

"Do you think he'll be all right, Nate? He told me heart problems run in your family."

"His doctor is one of the best; with a lot of attention and prayer, I think he'll be fine."

She averted her gaze and scoffed. "Prayer. For the life of me, I can't understand why he prays to a God who obviously doesn't care. He didn't care about Brian getting beat up by his dad all those years or later having no dad."

Nate felt an odd sense of déjà vu, remembering a similar conversation with Carly. He hesitated, not wanting to spend more time with Julia than he had to, but the sense that he should talk to her remained, and he led her to a private waiting area. He told her much of what he'd told Carly, surprised when Julia not only listened but then quietly asked him to keep praying for all of them. Her request was brief and tense, but he felt she'd meant it.

Later, in his dad's room, Nate realized with shock that sharp edges no longer bordered his thoughts concerning Julia or even Brian. Something had happened to Nate on the trail to eliminate the anger, and he attributed the reason to knowing Carly.

"Are you all right, son?" his dad asked when Nate continued staring into space.

Nate lifted his brows. "The question seems reversed. Shouldn't I be asking you that?"

His dad smiled.

"I'm sorry I wasn't here for you." Nate's guilt weighed heavily on his heart.

"Here for me?"

"When this happened."

"Nonsense." His dad shook it off.

"No, really. I should have been here."

"Nate, I've thought a good deal about our last conversation. You're a grown man. I expect you to live your own life and not feel as if you have to stay in Bridgedale to watch out for me."

"Stay in Bridgedale?" Nate was shocked. "What are you talking about?"

"I've sensed for some time you would like to spread your wings, like Nina has done. You always were the type to get restless if you stayed anywhere for long, probably because we made so many moves when you were a boy."

"Yeah, but move away from Bridgedale?"

"You don't like it here; that's obvious. So don't stay. There are plenty of nice cities and towns in Vermont; you don't have to go far." His dad grew reflective. "I especially liked that small town we lived in when you and Nina were in high school—Goosebury. Now there's a name if ever I heard one." He chuckled, then winced.

An odd sense of fate led Nate to say, "Strange you should bring up Goosebury. The group I hiked with was from there."

"Really? Anyone I know?"

"Ted Lizacek and his wife. . .you remember, I went to school with him."

"The name does ring a bell."

It should; Nate had practically lived at Ted's home.

"A honeymooning couple that lives outside of Goosebury, and some newcomers to the area—a man and his teenaged daughter. And Carly Alden."

"Alden." His father's eyes brightened. "The same Alden that formed the Covered Bridge Society there?"

"I don't know. I guess. She lives with an uncle and aunt."

"I seem to remember him mentioning a niece." His father peered at his face. "So are you interested in this girl?"

Nate's shock vibrated to his spine. "What makes you ask that?"

"She's the only one you mentioned by name besides Ted."

His dad was too keen. "It wouldn't matter if I was."

"Oh? Why is that?"

"You told me not to make the same mistakes you did, and I'm taking your advice."

"I see." Understanding filled his father's eyes. "I'm sorry for you but am glad to hear it, son."

"Actually, as long as we're on this subject, I need to get something off my chest." Nate hesitated, not wanting to upset his father but knowing he needed to acknowledge past mistakes. "I judged you for marrying Julia; if nothing else, my experience with Carly taught me that what we're so ready to condemn others for, often without understanding the situation firsthand, can wind up being our own personal temptation."

"Unless you've walked a mile in a man's shoes, don't fault him for stumbling when the path gets rocky?"

Nate chuckled in wry agreement. "Yeah, something like that."

He felt better for having spoken, and the two men shared an understanding smile.

fifteen

After a steep and rocky trek, Carly and the others made it to Shooting Star Shelter. Surprised to see another hiker there when the trail had seemed abandoned by all but them, they eagerly welcomed the older gentleman into their circle. From his radio, they learned that the man who'd murdered the two hikers had been found and brought into custody, and everyone rested easier that night. All except Carly.

She wandered the fringes of the camp to seek some solitude and realized with a wry twist that she missed the way Nate always found her. Taking a seat on the ground, she stared up at the starry sky, intent on spying out the constellations. Even they weren't random but formed pictures, appearing to tell a story. She remembered how Sierra once said that God wrote His story in the heavens at the very dawn of creation. For a moment, Carly wondered about her ancient ancestor, chief to the Abenaki, and if he'd sat on this very mountain studying the stars, pondering their story.

She thought about her own story: abandoned, misplaced, ignored. Was it any wonder she felt separated from everyone else, that God wouldn't want her either? Years ago, she had stopped feeling sorry for herself. She had attributed her breakdowns with Nate to utter exhaustion. Yet while these weeks had broken her, they had helped build her up, too. The book Nate had given her. . .the words seemed to niggle inside whatever was left of Carly's wall, urging her to come out from behind the old bitterness, the old pain, and to accept the teachings on the pages.

With absent movements, she shuffled the book's edges with her fingers, listening to the pages riffle. She thought about the message the book held that made more sense than she would have believed possible; she thought about her friends who showed such courage through their problems and attributed their strength to their relationships with God; she thought about Nate, who'd become more than a friend and had been forthright in his answers, never pretending something he didn't know. But most of all, she thought about what Jesus had said in Matthew when He instructed His disciples before He left them: "I am with you always, even unto the end of the world." Nate felt it; Kim felt it; Jill felt it; Leslie felt it. All of them were assured of the message and harbored no doubt. They trusted God's Word.

Jill told her last night that the Lord had never let her down, and when—just as a child who didn't understand a parent's decisions or rules—she felt God had failed her, He always comforted her, showing His love in different ways. Carly thought about what life might have been like if her mother hadn't dumped her on Aunt Dorothy. She'd been raised without love but had never wanted for anything material. She'd been given a good education, along with her younger cousin. For the first time, Carly acknowledged that if her mother had kept her, she may have suffered a much worse existence than she had. Now she could see it was better for her that her childish prayer had never been answered.

How long she sat there before she heard footsteps, Carly didn't know. Possibly hours.

Kim sat down beside her. "Is everything all right?" Her eyes were sleepy behind the glasses, and Carly realized the teenager must have just woken up. Once Kim had confided in her regarding a very personal matter; now Carly chose to do the same.

"Kim, how does one become a Christian?"

Taken aback, the girl blinked. "Well, um, okay. You pray and ask Jesus to come into your heart. And you should also ask Him to forgive you for your sins. That's what I did."

Heart pounding, Carly nodded. She needed no further contemplation. Ever since she'd sat down tonight, she'd known this moment had arrived. Tomorrow would take them to the end of the trail, but on this night, Carly decided to travel a new path to what she sensed would be the start of a lifelong adventure.

"Will you help me?"

At Carly's soft question, Kim smiled and took hold of her hands as the group had always done before prayer; while above them, the stars glimmered in a peaceful sky, silently telling their Creator's story.

❧

Nate spent most of his time at the hospital until the day of his father's release; then he went home to sort out his own life. Looking around his shabby apartment, he realized his dad had been right. Nate was tired of Bridgedale, but he wasn't sure where to go. Not Goosebury, that was a given.

As the weeks slid by, the pain of losing touch with Carly grew less intense. He still missed her and prayed for her, but he felt assured God would give him the strength needed to go on. He felt emotionally weary, like a survivor of a battle or as if he'd passed some sort of endurance test. In hindsight, that he had passed gave him relief. Twice, he almost e-mailed Ted to ask about Carly but resisted, deciding it better not to invite heartache or temptation back into his life.

The townspeople hadn't changed their views toward him and his family, though their words and looks were less aggressive. His church seemed more sympathetic; and though he hadn't spent time in outside activities with its members, tonight he planned to attend a singles' dinner.

He looked over his stack of mail, curious when he saw a letter from Jill. He tore into it and withdrew a sheet of paper. On it were all the names, addresses, e-mail addresses, and phone numbers of everyone who'd been in their hiking group, along with a brief note from Jill about how she thought it a good idea if they all stayed in touch.

Nate spotted Carly's name immediately, followed by numbers that told how to reach her. He ran his finger along the line of them, finding that he had sudden trouble breathing, and he stared at the paper a long time. His hands shook as he crumpled the page into a ball and tossed it toward the wastebasket. Tossed it and missed.

Rather than pick it up, he grabbed his jacket and keys and left his apartment as though a fire alarm had gone off in the building as well as inside his brain.

❧

"Rack 'em." Sierra gave Bart a wicked grin as she rolled the eight ball down the table his way.

"That's right. Rub it in," he muttered.

Carly chuckled as she chalked her cue stick, bending over the table and poising herself to break for their second game against the guys. At the loud smack, the colored balls scattered, sinking a solid in the corner. She scoped out the table. "Three in the side, six in the corner," she said before hitting the cue ball with expert precision. The red and green balls shot to their respective pockets.

"Good onya!" Jill cried.

"Well done," Leslie agreed.

Carly again ran the table. Ted groaned, and Jill laughed.

"If you weren't before, you blokes are sooo lost now," she teased. "We have a pro on our side, and we're going to cream you!"

Jill literally glowed. All in their group had been shocked and excited to hear upon their return to Goosebury that her bouts of illness had been due to being pregnant. Carly realized more than ever how God had protected her friend, since Jill had only endured minor falls on the trail.

"If only Nate were here," Ted grumbled. "Talk about a pro; he was a pool shark in high school. We won many a game in those days."

Upon hearing Nate's name, Carly lost all concentration and missed her mark. The cue ball smacked into the wrong one and bounced off the rim, narrowly knocking the eight ball in the corner pocket and losing them the game.

"Careful, Carly," Leslie said from her stool by the wet bar, where sodas and chips had been laid out.

"Too right," Jill added.

Carly walked over to Leslie. "I slipped." She shrugged.

"Yeah, and I bet I know why." Leslie cast a look at Blaine, who stood busy, selecting a cue stick from a rack on the wall. "Jill told me about you and Nate. I'm not sure what surprised me more—that you fell so hard and so fast for him or that Nate was the guy I had a crush on in high school. We went to the same one, you know."

"You never told me that." Carly looked at Leslie, amazed. She had been four grades behind Leslie so had never known Leslie or her classmates.

"I didn't know her Nate and my Nate were the same. Anyhow, it wasn't something I wanted to broadcast. Nate and I were the innocent parties to the brunt of a practical joke set up to hurt me by another girl who liked him. Actually, just about every girl in high school liked him. It was a black day when his family moved from Goosebury." Leslie laughed.

"I figured he was popular." Carly watched Blaine take a shot, though her mind didn't follow the game.

"Have you e-mailed him?"

"Why would I do that?"

"How about because you like him? And there are no longer any obstacles—" Leslie cut short her words, as if she shouldn't have said what she did.

"Obstacles? What do you mean?"

Leslie wet her lips. "Maybe I shouldn't have said anything, but now that you're a Christian, you should know. The Bible warns us not to have a relationship with anyone who doesn't share our faith—simply because it can pull us back and make us fall away from God. It's not to be mean or anything, or like we think we're better than others. We just have to be careful so as not to lose what we've found."

Carly's mind swam at Leslie's words. She had thought that Nate hadn't contacted her because he wasn't interested in anything more than friendship; his farewell had been final enough. It had hurt, still hurt, but Carly was learning to accept it. Thinking back, she realized his distance and odd behavior came after she'd told him she didn't believe in God. Now Jill's remarks about a recent blunder and about her wanting Carly and Nate only to be "good mates" made sense, too.

She had come so far since that night. If she'd known about the peace and satisfaction that came once she accepted Christ, she might have searched for answers long ago. Then again, she'd always been pretty hard-nosed. It had taken quite a few knocks on the trail to shake her up enough to get her to listen.

"Oh!" Leslie pressed a hand to her distended stomach.

At her sharp exclamation, Blaine scratched, his cue stick skidding across the green felt and sending the eight ball into the corner pocket.

"Leslie?" He approached his wife, his face white.

She nodded with a small, scared smile. "It's time."

"But you're not due for another two weeks." Blaine looked as if he might pass out or be sick. He put a shaky hand to her back. "Maybe it's just false labor pains, hon, like last time."

Carly glanced down, noticing the material of Leslie's brown jumper had darkened. "Not this time, Blaine. Her water just broke."

Blaine's face went almost gray. Everyone jumped into frenzied action, and somehow Blaine found the strength needed to keep it together and assist his wife upstairs and into their car. Jill called the doctor, and Carly took the house key Blaine pushed into her hand to go and grab Leslie's things and bring them to the hospital, while Sierra called the church prayer team on her cell phone.

Once Carly made it to Blaine and Leslie's house and found the already-packed case in the front room, she hurried back to her car. By the time she arrived at the hospital, she noticed Ted and Bart doing their level best to try to keep Blaine from losing it. She had a lot of time to think about all Leslie had revealed, and in between prayers for her friend, she made her decision.

sixteen

The next morning, after a night of little sleep in an uncomfortable chair, Carly drove home, tired and cranky. She let herself in the front door.

"Where have you been all night?" Aunt Dorothy asked sternly. "Up to no good. I'd stake my life on it."

"Then you would be dead." Carly had noticed her cousin's bike missing from the garage, so she felt it safe to speak. "I was at the hospital; Leslie went into labor last night and had a baby this morning—a girl. Seven pounds, eight ounces." Carly delivered her words in a monotone, her thoughts jumping ahead. "Now I have a question I'd like answered."

Her aunt's facial muscles tensed.

"Why do you hate me so much?"

Aunt Dorothy closed her mouth, looking away. Hearing footsteps, Carly turned to look as her uncle came from the kitchen, his newspaper still in hand.

"Is it because I'm his daughter?"

Her aunt gave a sharp intake of breath, but her uncle's expression told Carly what she needed to know. Shock, followed by a strange mix of remorse and relief gentled his brown eyes.

Carly gave a stiff nod. "I thought so." Without another word, she trudged upstairs to her attic room.

She sat on the bed and stared at the wall, barely aware of the tap at her door. She turned to find it slowly opening, her uncle on the threshold. They stared at one another as the old-fashioned clock on her bedside table ticked away the seconds.

He stepped inside, looking awkward. "We thought it best

not to tell you until you were grown. Later, we decided not to tell you at all."

Numb, Carly hugged herself and nodded.

"We didn't think Dorothy could have children; when your mother asked us to take you in, she agreed."

"And you?" She nailed him with a look. "Did you even want me?"

"I caused so much pain to both Dorothy and your mom; I only wanted what was best for everyone involved." He hesitated, then walked closer to sit down next to her. "But especially you. You were the innocent in all this."

Carly snorted. "Not according to Aunt Dorothy!"

"She's very bitter, and I honored her wish that you not be told. But Carly. . ." He moved as if he would take her hand, then sat back as if he'd changed his mind. "I have always cared and wanted what's best for you. I know I've been stern with you and not the best of uncles—we don't see eye to eye a lot of the time because we're too much alike. But if I hadn't cared about you all these years. . ."

"It's okay. You don't have to say it." Carly felt uneasy at this switch in their relationship, though she'd always suspected it.

He blew out a heavy breath. "That may be, but it's something I should have said long ago. You're special to me, Carly, my firstborn. I even had a hand in naming you, more or less."

Carly wasn't sure how much longer she could hold herself together and didn't respond, hoping he would go away. Yet this had been something she'd always wanted, to know her father, to talk to him.

He must have read the pain-filled indecision on her face. "It appears to me this isn't a good time, but now that you know the truth, we need to talk. We can go to Milton's Pantry and discuss things over dinner this weekend."

She had to know. "Were you ever planning to tell me the

truth? Or would you have been content just to go on pretending you were my uncle?"

"As a matter of fact, Dorothy and I have argued about this for a long time. I felt you should know when you hit twenty-one, but I refrained from saying anything then. Now, at least that disagreement between us has been settled."

"I don't want Trina knowing." Carly made the decision. She didn't want her little cousin's hatred, too.

He sighed. "Let's just take this as it comes. This past hour has been full enough already."

Carly nodded, watching distantly as he patted her hand, then rose and left the room. She swiped away the tears that dripped down her cheeks. Though she felt tired, she needed action, and she knew she would never be able to sleep.

Moving to her desk, Carly turned on her computer to check her e-mail. A brief, lighthearted post bursting with smiley faces, hearts, and dancing animated kittens and puppies came from Kim, and Carly smiled. When they'd crossed the Canadian border at the end of the trail, even as weary as all of them were, Kim had thrown off her backpack and done a series of cartwheels, exuberant that she'd made it to the end—that she'd lived out her dream.

Carly dashed off an equally silly reply to the teen's post, sent it, and tapped her finger against the keyboard, deep in thought. Piercing the corner of her lip with her teeth, she looked at the folded page Jill had given her at church weeks earlier.

"Come on, Carly girl," she muttered to herself. "Where's your backbone? You just braved your aunt with a question that's revolved inside your head for years and discovered the truth. This could never be as bad."

She hoped.

Smoothing out the page, she spotted Nate's address and began to type.

Nate packed up the last of the moving cartons, glad to be getting out of the dump he'd called his apartment for a year. He was taking to the road, uncertain of his destination and planning to wing it. Once he found a place he liked, he might settle. He winced when the telephone rang—again—and Brittany left her sixth message. He'd met her at the singles' dinner weeks earlier, had taken her out twice, but knew it wouldn't lead anywhere and had tried to tell her so. But she wouldn't listen. Nor, it seemed, would Susan, who now wanted back in his life and called just as often.

Glancing at his laptop, he wondered if he should boot up one final time and check his e-mail in case anyone had contacted him from the hiking group. He mocked himself.

"What for? You don't need to hear from her; you don't want to hear from her. Remember?" Besides, if she did contact him and he learned she still hadn't found Christ, it might kill him. He wondered just how long it would take for these feelings to dissolve.

Spotting a library book he'd checked out during his quest of deciding where to go—one filled with information on Vermont's towns—he groaned. He should drop it off before he forgot and maybe pick up a fast-food meal on the way. After all that packing, he was hungry.

Twenty minutes later, library book in hand, he approached the front desk. The young librarian smiled at him as he handed her the book.

"Yoo-hoo, Nate!"

At the loud stage whisper, he looked into the adjoining glassed-in room where a few computers sat at a long table— and also Mrs. Greenwich, the keyboard player at his church.

"I'm so glad to see you. Be a dear and watch this for me, will you?"

Puzzled, Nate pulled his brows together. "You want me to watch a computer?"

"Yes, I have to make a quick trip to the ladies room, and those school boys over there jump on whenever a computer is unmanned and no one's looking. We're on a scheduled time with these you know. I don't want to lose my slot or my article."

"Sure, okay." He glanced at the open screen of the Internet article she'd been reading about crochet patterns.

"Feel free to use it while I'm gone—just don't lose my window."

Once she'd left, he stared at the screen, tempted to look at his e-mail account. Loud whispers and muffled laughter drew Nate's attention to the three boys—brothers, judging from their red hair. They pretended to pore over a book, and as Nate watched, one of the boys made spitwads from his notebook paper on the table and stuck it in a straw. Nate shook his head as one of the paper cannonballs went flying into an unlucky bystander's hair. The boys fairly fell over themselves with quiet laughter as the woman continued to peruse the books, heedless that a white glob sat in her teased, sprayed hair. A stern, elderly librarian approached the table, and the boys quickly behaved like docile angels, again poring over the book.

Nate shook his head at their antics and glanced at the computer screen again, then at the keyboard. As long as he was here and the thing was sitting in front of him, why not look?

He opened a new window and brought up his e-mail account, his eyes going wide when he saw he had a post from Carly. His heart tapped out a crazy dance, and he felt as if he were caught up in some slow-moving dream as he moved the mouse to click her message open.

"I told you I'd be back in a flash," Mrs. Greenwich suddenly said as she approached him.

Nate quickly closed the window and rose from the chair.

"Thanks for watching things. Will we be seeing you at church this Sunday? It's so lovely you could make it to the singles' outings. My Joey enjoys them so, and from what he said, it appears to me that girl Brittany likes you."

He refrained from wincing at her obvious attempt at matchmaking. "No, actually I'm leaving town tomorrow."

"Is that a fact?"

Nate smiled. "I'm going to see a little of the world—Vermont anyhow. I need to get back to packing. Good-bye, Mrs. Greenwich."

Nate moved toward the front doors, his curiosity heightened by Carly's post. If he hadn't wasted time watching those unruly boys, he would have had a chance to read it. What could she have to say to him? What did she want? It had been almost a month and a half since they'd parted ways, and she'd never written before this.

Nate toyed with the idea of signing up for some Internet time to check it out. But he didn't want to get sucked into a lengthy conversation about Brittany or his family with Mrs. Greenwich, and Mrs. G was, as Jill would say, a real ear basher. The woman loved to talk up a storm.

Exiting the library, Nate shook his head at his stupidity of how easily he'd almost fallen into the trap of reopening contact with Carly.

seventeen

"Bases are loaded," Carly whispered to Kim. "This is a sure thing; don't sweat it. Remember, she pitches low and fast."

Kim nodded, adjusted her cap, and took up the bat. In the past three weeks, her vision had worsened, but the kid was a fighter and determined to enjoy life, even, she'd told Carly, after the blindness struck. She'd taught herself Braille and confided to Carly that with the new Braille deck of cards her father had bought her, she would continue whipping Carly at their games. In turn, Carly taught Kim expert tips in shooting pool after Wednesday night Bible studies and assured Kim that somehow she would help her learn to knock the right balls in their pockets and obliterate the guys each game, even after her sight was gone.

Now an assistant softball coach for her church's team, Carly watched Kim step up to the plate to practice her swing. Ted, the real head honcho, employed his usual tactics to whip the team into shape at practice.

"Come on, Sasha," Carly yelled to the nineteen-year-old who ran for second base once Kim hit the ball far outfield. "Come on! Pick up those heels, woman! This isn't a turtle race."

"I see our drill sarge's bad habits rubbed off on you."

Carly froze at the voice she'd thought never to hear again.

As Marissa slid into home plate, barely missing being tagged as the third out, Carly gave the girl no more acknowledgment for her nimble feat than a dazed nod. When she felt she could turn around, Carly looked beyond the fence.

Nate stood there, a few feet away, as attractive as ever in a blue T-shirt and jeans. His eyes reflected the sky; his smile was as calm as the breeze. Carly had to remind herself to breathe.

"Carly—watch out!"

Before she could move, what felt like a boulder struck between her shoulders. "Oof!" This time she really fought for breath as she bent over double, grabbing her knees, and Sasha, along with Kim and a few other team members ran from their places on the field and surrounded her. "You okay, Carly?" Kim asked.

"Whoever called it a 'soft' ball didn't know what they were talking about," she muttered when she could talk.

"Sorry, Carly!" Loretta, an outfielder and one of the worst ball players in all of Goosebury, called out.

All at once, large, warm hands grasped Carly's shoulders, and he was there with her. "Come on and sit down." Nate led her to the ballpark's row of bleachers. "Looks like your trail mate is to the rescue—again."

She almost laughed but for the pain it caused. Leslie handed her baby girl, Marena, to Blaine and hurried Carly's way. "I saw the whole thing from the car. We just got here. Let's go to the rest room and take a look at the damage."

Carly hesitated, looking at Nate.

"I'm not going anywhere."

His intense blue-gray eyes sent a shiver of expectation through her, and minutes later, his steady words rang through her mind while she stood before the sink. Leslie pulled up her shirt and studied her back. "Ouch. You're going to have quite a bruise, but I think you'll live. Do you want me to get some ice?"

"And just how would I hold it there?"

"Good point. Maybe you should call it a day and go home. Soak in a tub?"

Carly heard the teasing in Leslie's voice. As many times as Carly had tormented Leslie when she'd dated Blaine, Carly deserved her friend's treatment. Their eyes met in the mirror.

"Why do you think he came back?" Carly questioned.

"Why don't you ask him?"

"Would it bother you much?"

"What do you mean?"

"Since you liked him in high school. I mean, on the off chance something did happen, I wouldn't want you to be uncomfortable around me, us. With all that happened with you two." Good grief. She was blabbering like a smitten kid and making no sense whatsoever.

Leslie laughed. "Nothing happened. I doubt he even remembers me; we shared a few classes, that's all. But those days are long gone, Carly. I'm a happily married woman, in love with my husband, not a jealous teen sulking over an old high school crush." She winked. "I say go for it."

Carly grinned. "If I don't hyperventilate this time or have the dugout fall on top of me, I just might. But first, I want to hear what he has to say. He has a lot of explaining to do."

Leslie chuckled, shaking her head. "I sure don't envy Nate right now."

૨

Nate perched on the bleachers, awaiting Carly's return. He had opened her e-mail message two days ago, unable to resist anymore knowing what she had to say. In her brief message, she had inquired after him and his family and stated that she hoped his father was well. She had added in a postscript—"Oh, by the way, I dug into your book and found all the info needed. With Kim's help, I accepted Christ the day before we hit Canada. Thanks for all your patience and help. Without you as my trail mate, I would have never reached that end goal."

Blown away, Nate had stared at his computer screen for endless moments before scrambling for his cell phone to call Ted, who confirmed Carly's words and that she'd also joined their church.

A flash of bright red brought his attention to Carly and her friend walking his way. The woman spoke to Carly, then joined a man holding a baby. Nate studied Carly. As beautiful as ever, she approached him. His heart beat as if it weren't a part of his body, just as it had done when he'd first spotted Carly near home plate giving Kim advice.

Washed in bright sunlight, her flawless skin held a healthy glow, and he detected a sparkle in her dark eyes. She had pulled her hair back in a long, messy ponytail and stuffed it under the red ball cap.

"Is everything all right?" he asked when she took a seat on the bleachers beside him.

"After a month of mishaps on the Long Trail, this is nothing."

He looked into her curious eyes, recognizing her reference to their time together as a question, an invitation to proceed with what had brought him to her.

"I got your e-mail, Carly. I'm glad you made the choice you did."

"So am I. I'm sorry to hear your service is so slow, though."

"Slow?"

"Your e-mail account. I sent that post weeks ago."

He bit back a wry grin. So that's how it was going to be. "I moved out of Bridgedale and have been on the road for weeks, not always near a computer. I had a lot of decisions to make; a lot of praying to do."

She mulled that over and smiled, her expression relaxing. "I understand. I've done a lot of that lately, too."

To hear proof of her practicing her faith cheered him.

"You look good. Are things going better for you?"

"Some things. I discovered I was right about my uncle—he is my father. We had a rough few days, but we're sorting it all out. Jake visited a few times while we were hiking. I think he decided I'd moved away; he hasn't bothered me since."

"That's good to hear."

"And I've been writing my guidebook. I'm still not sure if I'm going anywhere with that, but I directed Cat to a magazine publisher who showed interest in some of her poems."

"That's terrific. So, do you like this church?"

"I love it. I felt as if I belonged from the moment I stepped foot inside the door with Les."

"Les?" Alarm shot through Nate.

"Leslie Cartell, my friend." She motioned to the woman with the baby. "A nickname I call her."

"You and your nicknames." Relief made him smile. "Do you have your mini recorder with you?"

"It's in my car," she said, her tone confused.

He nodded, thinking. "So do you need to stay until the game is over?"

Her eyes grew wider. "No, I can leave. This is only a practice game." She glanced at the coach, and Nate looked, too. Ted caught their looks and made a sweeping, umpire-like motion with both arms, pointing to the parking lot.

Carly chuckled. "Mr. Subtlety has spoken."

Nate grinned. "Let's get out of here." He noticed Carly wince as she stood up. "Maybe you should have that looked at."

"I'm okay, just sore."

"Have you eaten?"

"I had an apple before the game."

"Let's get something to eat. I haven't eaten since breakfast." She looked at him, her eyes brimming with questions, but he needed to do this his way.

They stopped at her car first so she could grab her recorder from the glove compartment. Nate opened the passenger door of his car, not failing to note her confusion before she slid inside. Neither of them spoke during the five-block drive to a fast-food restaurant. Nate pulled into the drive-through area and looked at the menu.

"Nothing much for a veggie lover, but they have a cucumber salad."

"I'll just take French fries and a vanilla shake." She pulled off her ball cap, setting it in her lap.

Nate heard the quiver in her voice; his own insides shook, and he wondered if eating a hamburger was a wise choice. Once they received their order, he drove to another area of the park. They shared a bench and small talk while they ate and watched the ducks glide on the quiet, glassy pond.

As Carly gathered her trash and stuck it in the bag, she winced.

"Turn around, Carly."

"Why?" she asked but did as he quietly ordered, swinging her legs to the edge of the bench.

Nate slid closer and pushed her long ponytail over her shoulder, then lifted his jumbo cup of iced soda to the middle of her upper back. She gave a sharp intake of breath as soon as he touched her, and he sensed it wasn't the extreme cold against her T-shirt that caused her sudden shortness of breath. His own pulse had sped up at the silky texture of her hair against his fingers.

"Better?" he whispered.

She gave a weak response that sounded like confirmation.

"I imagine you're wondering why I'm in Goosebury," he said after a moment, knowing the time had come to speak.

"The thought had crossed my mind."

"I came to give you an interview. An exclusive."

"An interview?"

He sensed disappointment in her puzzled question.

"Ted told me you still haven't found a job. This will guarantee you a top position in the best newspaper office in all of Goosebury. A hot and juicy headliner, just like you always wanted."

She remained so quiet he wished he could see her face.

"Turn your recorder on, Carly."

He noticed her hand shake as she did.

"My name is Nate Bigelow. Brian Bigelow is my stepbrother. My father adopted him when he married my stepmother."

She gave another sharp intake of breath.

"I see you recognize the name." He let out a soft snort. "For months the local press, the national news, the news magazines have hounded my family for the inside scoop, but we've managed to avoid them. Now I want to give you the story. Everything you want to know."

He lowered his drink from her back as she slowly turned on the bench to look at him. She switched off the recorder button. "Why, Nate? Why me?"

"That's a question I'd prefer to answer after the interview. Shall we continue?"

She nodded, still dazed, but he saw her journalistic brain move into gear as her eyes grew more alert, and she began to call the shots.

"First, why don't you tell me about your relationship with Brian, how long you've known him, and anything else you feel might be significant?" she suggested, switching her recorder back on.

For the next fifteen minutes, Nate recounted everything from the time he'd met his troubled young stepbrother when his dad dated Julia to the time of the crime. Afterward, he answered each of Carly's soft questions, more often about him than Brian, until she could think of nothing more to ask. She turned off the recorder and studied him. This had been the part he'd been dreading ever since he'd decided to do this interview.

"Now that you know the truth about my family, how do you feel about me, Carly?"

"Feel about you?" His question clearly baffled her. "No different than usual. . .why?"

Nate's heart skipped a beat at her answer and then began to pick up speed. "And what is 'usual'?"

He was asking a lot from her, and he knew it by the cautious look that entered her eyes. She remained silent, but her silence was all the answer he needed.

"My stay in Goosebury is permanent," he admitted. "I moved here a few days ago."

Her eyes widened, her lips parted. "Oh."

"And if you're willing, I'd like for us to become more than trail mates."

"Oh." The word left her mouth in a whoosh. He didn't miss the way her eyes lit up. He waited for her to say more.

She swallowed and moistened her lips. "Since you've avoided interviews for so long, why'd you give me the story, Nate?"

"Isn't it obvious? What other information do you need to figure it out?"

"I'm a bit slow on the uptake today," she whispered. "Maybe you should just tell me?"

He skimmed his fingertips down her cheek. "How about if I show you instead? I love you, Carly; I have for some time."

He lowered his head and caught her gasp with his mouth as he gave in to his overwhelming desire to kiss her. His own breath wedged inside his throat when she softly whimpered in relief and clutched his shoulders, eagerly returning his kiss.

With great effort, he drew away, having wanted this for so long and now realizing she'd wanted the same. "And I trust you," he whispered. "I know you won't twist my words, that you'll do the right thing with this interview."

Carly blinked several times as if to collect her thoughts, then gave a slight nod. To Nate's shock, she ejected the microcassette and dropped it into what was left of her vanilla shake.

"Why'd you do that?" His mouth dropped open.

"There's no garbage can nearby, and I don't want to litter." She shrugged as he continued to gape at her. "I could have just erased the tape, but I have a box of fifty at home, so losing one isn't so bad. And I wanted you to get the message."

"What message? That you like your mud shakes better than vanilla ones?"

She chuckled. "That you can trust me, Nate. With anything." When he only stared, she explained, "I haven't often done the right thing. Now that I have a clean slate, I don't want to muddy it up with a lot of dirt."

"Dirt?" She had completely lost him.

"Dirt. My own experiences showed me that some stories shouldn't be broadcasted. Sometimes the public doesn't need to know all of the gruesome details or the dark background facts, and I think this is one of those times." She smiled.

"But what about the job you've always wanted as a top journalist?"

"If I can't get a job on my own merit and instead have to rely on someone else's pain and tragedy to further my career, then I'm not interested in pursuing it. I'd already planned to ditch the story halfway through our interview."

Dumbfounded, Nate expelled a confused, exasperated breath. "Then why'd you let me go on like that? Why'd you ask all those questions?"

"Isn't it obvious?" she teased, using his words from earlier. "I want to know everything there is to know about you, even the imperfect skeletons in your closet. After all, it's only fair." She grinned impishly. "You know mine."

"Carly." Nate shook his head in mystified amusement. "Will I ever understand you?"

"Probably not. But who knows what the future might hold?" Her eyes sparkled as she linked her arms around his neck. "Then, too, I've heard it said a little adventure can be fun." She pressed her lips to his.

All confusion fled Nate's mind as he wrapped his arms around her. He may never figure out this unpredictable, exciting, maddening woman, but he sure looked forward to the challenge of trying!

epilogue

Spring of the following year

Carly waited at the back of the church, her heart in her throat as she watched Kim carry her spring bouquet of pastel flowers down the aisle after Sierra. Kim had practiced the slow march for days, so as to make the procession without faltering and without the aid of her white cane. As she reached the front and turned gracefully to the left, Carly exhaled a relieved breath and silent cheer for her lovely young friend. She noticed Chris, a cousin of Nate's and the youngest of the groomsmen, watching Kim with the same intensity mixed with awe, and Carly smiled. Kim was now fifteen, Chris seventeen. From what Carly had witnessed these past weeks, she sensed young love in bloom. Kim's blindness hadn't deterred Chris one bit; he sought her company and acted very protective of her, though Kim's bubbly and confident nature seldom warranted such care.

Trina followed Kim, her head held high. Aunt Dorothy had just about died when Trina colored a violet streak in her dark hair to go with the rose dress, but Carly liked it. It suited her. Months ago, their father had decided to tell Trina that she and Carly were half sisters. For a few days, Trina had withdrawn, but she later approached Carly in her attic room and asked, "Since we're really sisters, does that mean I can have your CD collection when you die?" She had cracked a joking smile, and from that day forward, the two had grown even closer than before.

Jill squeezed Carly's arm. "No worries, luv." She winked in encouragement before taking her turn down the narrow aisle.

Leslie turned from her seat in the pew and smiled at both of them. She held Jill's infant son, Titus, and Blaine sat beside her, holding baby Marena, who was teething and gnawing on her daddy's shoulder. The dark-haired little beauty raised her head, catching sight of Carly in the floor-length, ice-white gown shot with iridescent sequins, and smiled, letting out a gurgling squeal. Blaine jiggled her to shush her, offering an apologetic look to Carly, who chuckled under her breath. Bart sat next to Blaine and gave her an emphatic thumbs-up. She felt so grateful to have all her friends there, and family, including her new one.

Carly's eyes went to the couple in the first pew. The trial pending, the Bigelows had visited Goosebury for a month's rest, and after meeting the distinguished lawyer, Carly had seen where his son had picked up many of his good traits, including his consideration for others.

As Jill moved down the aisle, Ted watched from where he stood at the front as best man. The drill sergeant, tough-as-nails coach made a surprisingly gentle and compassionate father to his son.

She had worried over whom to choose as her matron of honor, Jill or Leslie; both women were her dearest friends and had done so much for her. But when Leslie confided she was again pregnant and battled morning sickness, the decision became apparent.

Leslie had talked to her step-grandfather, who'd relented and allowed Carly a third chance at the *Gazette*. Within months, Carly proved her merit to Mr. Abernathy and became a top journalist assigned to some of the best stories. She had left the news office the first time ignorant but had returned with wisdom that gained favor with all those she interviewed—tenacity mixed with mercy.

Her father squeezed Carly's arm. "Are you ready?"

She smiled. "Are you kidding? I've been waiting for this day forever," she quipped, quoting one of Kim's lines.

Last night, her father had talked with Carly into the wee hours. With all subterfuge banished, the two of them had developed a close bond. She'd even witnessed to him about Christ on a few occasions, and he'd listened, showing interest. When she was little and dreamed of her prince charming, she'd wished she could have a daddy to one day walk her down the aisle, too. Now her dreams had become a reality. All of them.

The organist began the triumphant chords of Wagner's "Bridal Chorus" from *Lohengrin*, and Carly looked Nate's way, meeting his eyes. She worked to steady her suddenly rapid breathing and returned his expression of awe with a slight smile as she glided up to the altar to take her place beside him.

When Nate had asked her weeks ago why she'd never come up with a nickname for him, Carly had put her arm through his as they'd rocked on the porch glider. "I tried. But I never could settle on just one name because you're so many things to me. My Friend. My Trail Mate. My Rescuer. . ." At this she had rolled her eyes, and he had laughed. "My Brother in Christ. My Confidante. My Expert Pool-shark Partner." They both grinned, and then she grew serious. "My Love, and soon to be, My Husband. How can I come up with a nickname for all that?"

As the ceremony progressed and they spoke their vows to one another, Carly looked into Nate's sky-colored eyes glowing with love and wondered how she had ever gotten along without this man.

The minister pronounced them husband and wife, and the organ pealed a triumphant refrain. As Nate's mouth covered hers in a warm, intimate kiss, which sent her heart to the summits, Carly thanked God that from this day forward, she would have Nate as her lifelong trail mate.

And to her, that was better news than any headline story.

A Letter To Our Readers

Dear Reader:

In order that we might better contribute to your reading enjoyment, we would appreciate your taking a few minutes to respond to the following questions. We welcome your comments and read each form and letter we receive. When completed, please return to the following:

Fiction Editor
Heartsong Presents
PO Box 719
Uhrichsville, Ohio 44683

1. Did you enjoy reading *Long Trail to Love* by Pamela Griffin?
   ❏ Very much! I would like to see more books by this author!
   ❏ Moderately. I would have enjoyed it more if

   _____

   _____

   _____

2. Are you a member of **Heartsong Presents**? ❏ Yes ❏ No
   If no, where did you purchase this book? _____

   _____

3. How would you rate, on a scale from 1 (poor) to 5 (superior), the cover design? _____

4. On a scale from 1 (poor) to 10 (superior), please rate the following elements.

   ____ Heroine   ____ Plot
   ____ Hero   ____ Inspirational theme
   ____ Setting   ____ Secondary characters

5. These characters were special because? _____

_____

_____

6. How has this book inspired your life? _____

_____

_____

7. What settings would you like to see covered in future
   Heartsong Presents books? _____

_____

_____

8. What are some inspirational themes you would like to see
   treated in future books? _____

_____

_____

9. Would you be interested in reading other **Heartsong
   Presents** titles? ❏ Yes ❏ No

10. Please check your age range:
   ❏ Under 18   ❏ 18-24
   ❏ 25-34   ❏ 35-45
   ❏ 46-55   ❏ Over 55

Name _____

Occupation _____

Address _____

City, State, Zip_____

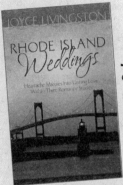

Presents